DEEP FREEZE

REVOLUTION

D.S. WEISSMAN

EPIC
Press

Revolution
Deep Freeze: Book #4

Written by D.S. Weissman

Published by EPIC Press™
PO Box 398166
Minneapolis, MN 55439

Cover design by Dorothy Toth
Images for cover art obtained from iStockPhoto.com
Edited by Melanie Austin

LIBRARY OF CONGRESS CATALOGING-IN-PUBLICATION DATA

Names: Weissman, D.S., author.
Title: Revolution / by D.S. Weissman.
Description: Minneapolis, MN : EPIC Press, [2017] | Series: Deep freeze ; book #4
Summary: As time passes, the settlement must maintain calm over the dwindling food supply
    and ever-worsening punishments. With the tension between the settlement and the newly
    formed outliers growing, the kids must choose whether they want to stay in the comforts of
    the settlement or chance freezing to death in the wild. Who they follow could be a choice
    between life and death.
Identifiers: LCCN 2015959460 | ISBN 9781680760187 (lib. bdg.) |
    ISBN 9781680762846 (ebook)
Subjects: LCSH: Adventure and adventurers—Fiction. | Interpersonal relationships—Fiction. |
    Survival—Fiction. | Human behavior—Fiction. | Young adult fiction.
Classification: DDC [Fic]—dc23
LC record available at http://lccn.loc.gov/2015959460

EPICPRESS.COM

To my friends, without whom I wouldn't have had the courage to write a book series to prove that I actually had a job

HOME IS FOR
THE HEART

TIC-TAC

Tic-Tac's father had made a habit of lighting his cigarettes on the stove. He also had a habit of trying to force Tic-Tac's stutter out with his fists. When Tic-Tac's parents were around, he kept all his answers to nods and headshakes. The less he spoke, the less embarrassed he felt, and the less he worried about his dad's violent episodes. Tic-Tac wondered if his father's anger stemmed from having once had a stutter. Did his father look at him and see a weaker version of himself?

The morning snuck in over the house. The sunlight filtered through the cracks and crust of Tic-Tac's window. He made his way to his sister's room and sat on her bed. She had caught the flu a few days earlier and rarely left her bed since. Her face was pale. Twice a day he helped change her sheets, which were soaked through with sweat and vomit. The night before, his mother had pressed her open hand to his sister's cheek and said "It's going to be okay."

His mother had left for work earlier that morning. Sometimes she left before sunrise and didn't return until long after dark. His father hadn't been to work in days, which meant he had lost another job. He sat around on the couch or tinkered in the garage on projects he swore he would finish soon. His father mostly moved around metal tools, clanked them together, and changed the oil on the old Camry; it was the most useful skill he had. This morning he had woken up the house, screaming that "that damn stove" was broken again.

Tic-Tac sat on his sister's bed and pressed his hand to her forehead.

"Nat-Nat—" he held his breath. It helped stop his uncontrollable repetition.

"It's like the hiccups," Natalie once said. "Try it for up to ten seconds."

Sometimes he had to try again when the same stammer continued; he puffed out his cheeks and felt flushed.

"You feel b-b-b-b—" he stopped again.

"It's okay," Natalie said. She made a strained but sincere smile. Her eyes were half closed. The doctor said the sickness needed to run its course. Tic-Tac helped to make sure she was hydrated. She looked sullen but not unhappy. Soon she would get out of bed and they would take the one-and-a-half-hour bus ride to the beach, make their way to the sand, and watch the surfers twist around the barrels.

The time he spent with his sister was his favorite. They could sit alongside one another in silence and say as much without words as others did with words. The waves would crash on the beach. People would throw footballs around the sand. Dogs would bark and nip at roller bladers. Seagulls would steal food out of people's hands. Tic-Tac and Natalie would sit at the center of it all, never wanting to leave.

"You feel b-b-b-b—" he tried again.

"Bet," she said. "One syllable at a time." Her voice was groggy and rough. Tic-Tac didn't know if it was from the sickness or the early morning. He pressed his lips together and paused. "Bet—ter," he said.

"Yes," she said. "I am feeling better. Get going to school."

"I'll c-c-c-c-come home after." He forced the last words out in a rush. People often jumped back from the force at which he spoke. Their reactions embarrassed him as much as the stutter.

She nodded. Tic-Tac didn't speak at school. His father's fists he could take; it was harder to take the ridicule of other children. He preferred to keep to himself and act like a ghost rather than pop like a firework when he couldn't complete a word. Whoever said "Sticks and stones can break your bones, but words can never hurt me" never met children who threw insults like rocks at a public stoning. Enough kids in Tic-Tac's class remembered him from second grade, before he knew his stutter wasn't normal. On slow days when the kids lacked entertainment and social niceties, they remembered Tic-Tac and the day he had stood up in front of the class and attempted to recite a line from the "Gettysburg Address."

"The brave men, living and d-d-d-d-d . . . " He had stood in front of a mirror for a week practicing the line over and over again, noting where he stuttered and stammered. He tried his hardest to keep the words from getting stuck on his lips. Natalie had seen him one afternoon, his brow furrowed, his eyes piercing the mirror, watching his throat.

"Why are you staring at your throat?" she asked.

"I thought I—" The words formed in his head, sat on his tongue, and stayed. "I-I-I . . . "

"You can do it."

"I-I saw wh . . . " He couldn't figure out the

disconnect between his mind and his mouth, his vocal cords and his thoughts. " . . . Where the words g-g-got stuck." He looked away from Natalie's reflection. *It was a stupid idea*, he thought.

"What are you doing?" she asked.

He showed her the Gettysburg Address.

"I remember doing that," she said. "Mr. Tibits?"

He nodded.

"Try bouncing into the lipped letters. The P's and the B's. The letters you press your lips together for. It's a short speech, at least. You need to do the whole thing?"

Tic-Tac shook his head.

"You can do it," Natalie said.

"Not likely," their dad said. Tic-Tac hadn't heard the garage door open. Natalie rolled her eyes.

"Leave him alone," she said.

"The day that kid recites the Gettysburg Address is the day I get my stock broker's license."

"I think one is far more likely," she said.

"Exactly," their dad said.

"I'm betting on you," she told Tic-Tac. "Go light another cigarette!" she said to their dad. She turned away and left Tic-Tac alone with his reflection.

Tic-Tac stopped in front of the class, held his breath for five seconds, and swallowed hard. Kids smelled fear the way bees and dogs did. They pointed and laughed, called him mumbling Matthew. Once a month Tic-Tac would play dodge-ball, or tag, or kickball, and a kid who thought himself clever would remind the class, screaming out "Mumbling Mat-Mat-Matthew!" to derail any semblance of normalcy Tic-Tac almost gained.

He survived another day without his voice. He had slunk into the corner of the classroom and disappeared. He drew his sister a card with a teddy bear on it. The teddy bear had an eye patch and held balloons. It had a word bubble above the bear that read, "Eye Can See You're Better." He colored it in with colored pencils. His sister didn't like the waxy build up from crayons. When Tic-Tac came home, his dad was asleep on the couch. The house smelled faintly of rotten eggs, but it wasn't the first time. A nearby natural gas electricity plant sometimes gave the neighborhood a spoiled smell. Tic-Tac went upstairs to his sister's room, sat on the edge of her bed, and handed her the card. Her cheeks were rosy. The sun forced its way through the crusted window and shined over the floor and walls in a pyramid of light. Used, crumpled tissues were scattered across her duvet.

"Thank you," Natalie said. "It looks exactly like Prudence." She held her teddy bear with both hands. "Except for the patch."

"It added c-c-character." Tic-Tac sniffed the air. "It smells like e-e-eggs."

"For Christ's sake!" their father screamed. He had woken up hungover from his mid-morning binge. If Tic-Tac went into the garage, he imagined he would find three different types of wrenches, two hammers, four screwdrivers, and an empty bottle of vodka spread over the floor. "Matthew, get down here!"

"Go," Natalie said. "You know how he gets."

Tic-Tac found his father in the kitchen with an unlit cigarette in his mouth. "You seen my lighter?" his father asked. "I can never find that thing."

His father twisted the nobs on the stove and bent over to light his cigarette on the flame, except the stove didn't light. One of the knobs hadn't moved at all. He kept his head close to the burner. The smell of gas was stronger in the kitchen. The cigarette dangled in his mouth. The stove clicked.

"This damn knob is stuck again." His father tapped at the knob but didn't try to move it. "You do your chores?"

Tic-Tac shook his head.

"You need to say something. You can't go through life shaking your head at things."

"No," Tic-Tac said. He stood in the doorway and saw his reflection in the window over the sink. His father peered at him.

"No, what?"

"No, s-s-s—" he cringed as his father's hand lashed out to slap him.

"We need to scare that damn thing out of you like the hiccups." He laughed and coughed. The cigarette bobbed in his mouth but clung to his dry lips. "Take out the trash. It smells like a rotten monkey's ass in here."

Tic-Tac grabbed the garbage bag. The stove's fumes leaked into the air. The scent of gas continued to fill the kitchen. The bag was heavy and wet. Few things smelled worse than wet garbage, except for hot, wet garbage. And possibly rotten eggs.

"Maybe you can find my damn lighter while you're at it," his father yelled. "We got any matches around here?" His father searched the drawers. Tic-Tac walked out of the house replacing the smell of gas with the smell of hot grass, wire fences, and the putrid garbage he tried to distance himself from. The asphalt waved in the heat. Beads of sweat formed on Tic-Tac's forehead. *This must be how Natalie feels*, he thought. He wanted to catch her sickness, crawl beneath his covers, and hide from his father in the comfort of his sheets, waiting for his mom to come home.

Sometimes his sister would stay home and read books, tucked in the nook of her bedroom. She would read the stories to him. She would go over the lines with him and try to teach him how to say the words without getting caught on them. She was patient and kind. She understood that he tried his best. When he made it through a sentence without a single stammer she praised him. When he couldn't do it, she encouraged him. He wanted to get upstairs and see what she read today.

Tic-Tac pulled the lid off the trashcan. He heaved the wet bag into the can and closed the lid. He held his nose to avoid the rotten garbage smell. The stagnant neighborhood filled with wind. The scent of gas was absent out here . . .

The silent air turned explosive. The house expanded in a burst of flame. The force heaved Tic-Tac over the trashcans and into the street. Wood shards rained down around him and clattered on the concrete. His head pounded with a million blows. Where was he? Why was the ground so hot? Why was the sky so far away? What happened to his head? He didn't know his father had left the stove on. He didn't know his dad lit a match after filling the kitchen with gas. Tic-Tac didn't know his mother would return to the remnants of their house, surrounded by fire trucks and paramedics, and break down, forever inconsolable.

The earth rang in his ears. Blood filled his mouth. His ribs ached when he breathed. He looked up to where his house had been and found remnants of his childhood scattered in pieces across the yard.

FORCED PLACEMENT

TIC-TAC

Tic-Tac WALKED THROUGH THE SQUARE IN THE OPEN NIGHT. Darkness overtook the settlement. Everyone slept, or pretended too. No one had seen the Northern Lights in months. Conversations in the dining hall always led to rumors. People said the lights disappeared the night James left, when he snuck past the howls of feral dogs.

"Abe didn't do it," Teagan had said earlier that night.

"That can't happen," Shia said.

"It sounds right to me," a thin-lipped girl said.

"Remember how Abe screamed when he found

17

out James was gone?" Teagan asked. "It pushed away the lights."

"It doesn't work that way," Shia said. But the rumor had started. *James would love to see how a rumor about himself snowballed*, Tic-Tac thought.

The dome stood at the fringe of the settlement, in silence. It hadn't been used since James killed Geoff. It seemed useless now, with its bars made of ice, a structure once damning, now impotent when not filled with bleeding kids. Every day, Tic-Tac had to walk past the Icedome. The haunted sounds of the ghosts that the dome had created—that the settlement had created—whispered in the light and cried in the darkness. Sarah hadn't wanted to be a part of it anymore. She had vacated her chair on the committee soon after James and Charlotte left. She had waited until Tic-Tac came back to their room one night, after he had crossed paths with the looming structure they all had built.

"It's too real," she'd said that night.

"What could that possibly even mean?" Tic-Tac

asked. His stutter was long gone. Sometimes Tic-Tac would go out of his way to use words he once had trouble saying, filling sentences with S's and P's. When he arrived in the Corral, he didn't speak in front of people and instead spent time at night in front of the bathroom mirror practicing phrases he thought he might say the following day.

"There was a moment when it all felt pretend," Sarah had said. "It was like when I used to sit and have a tea party with the girls in Fornland. There wasn't tea, there definitely wasn't a party, but we sat around acting like royalty asking someone to pass the cucumber sandwiches. When this whole thing started, it was like that. Whatever it is now doesn't feel that playful."

"That's because it isn't pretend," Tic-Tac said.

"It could have been."

Abe had replaced Sarah's seat on the committee that same day.

Tic-Tac continued his walk through the quiet snow-covered grounds. He had gone to check on

Autry and the greenhouse. Autry spent most of her days hiding in the humid company of plants. The soil looked healthy but Tic-Tac had to take Autry's word for how the plants should look. He never knew much about botany.

"Please," Rachel said. "Help me."

Rachel was tied to a wooden post in the heart of the central square. What was left of her clothes was tattered. Her teeth chattered. Her skin looked blue in the dim glow of candles that flickered through the windows. Crusty blood froze to her cheeks, her wrists, between her nose and her lips. The cold air dried her skin, shrinking it until it cracked open. The rules of the settlement changed once James left, and no one said a word, including Tic-Tac.

"I swear I didn't do anything," Rachel said.

She had been accused of helping James and the outliers, giving them food and clothing, heat, candles, whatever they needed, whatever she could take. She had stood at the center of the committee with her eyes cast to her bare feet. Her hair was stringy but clean. Abe led the meeting, and Tic-Tac sat to Abe's left, as the intermediary between Abe and the rest of the settlement. Shia sat on Abe's right, and two new kids, Andrew and Kelsey, had replaced James and Charlotte. After Geoff died, they decided to keep that seat open.

Abe said it commemorated Geoff's sacrifice. In the quiet whispers of the committee, Abe revealed he didn't want to replace Elise's chair. The settlement said the seat was haunted, perpetuating a myth that anyone who sat in Elise's old chair would die.

Since James left, people filled their active minds with rumors instead of the tales James had told. Tic-Tac wasn't sure if the rumor mill had been this active before James left or if the settlement craved a story so dearly they would make up anything hoping for truth. He didn't believe Elise's seat on the committee was haunted, but why take the chance?

Tic-Tac felt a pang of sadness whenever he walked into the building and saw Elise's chair empty and Sarah's filled. He had hoped she would change her mind and come back. He knew her well enough to know she wouldn't, but it didn't stop him from wanting it to happen. Whatever sense of levity had filled their lives for a short while couldn't be found with a microscope these days.

When Rachel stood in the room not looking at anyone, Abe had his middle finger pressed to his lips. He struck the pose more often now. His index finger had turned black and started to reek of hot garbage. Abe hid the finger from everyone. It wasn't hard to notice. Abe would keep his voice low when he spoke. Any verve and animation he once had was lost.

"You have been accused of helping the outliers," Abe said.

"I haven't done—" Rachel said.

"Don't speak," Abe said with quiet calm. "You'll know when it's your turn." She nodded and returned her eyes to the floor. Her hair stayed motionless around her face. *She could have been a witch in a different life*, Tic-Tac thought, *if this was a different story.*

Tic-Tac tried not to look at her. A number of kids had recently stood in the committee, each one cited for infractions witnessed by some obscure character Abe said had "confided" in him under the promise of anonymity. Since James and Charlotte had left, the settlement looked darker, seemed harsher, and lost some of the lighthearted life that once swirled around, even in the bad times. Now it felt like the settlement was built underneath flimsy icicles—any wrong step would get them impaled.

"Is it true you were on kitchen duty last night?" Kelsey asked. Her accusatory tone made Tic-Tac squeeze his fist. Whenever he felt compelled to say something he often dug his nails into his palms and concentrated on the sting in his skin.

"I wasn't the only—" Rachel said.

"It isn't your turn yet," Abe said.

"How can she respond if she isn't allowed to talk?" Shia asked. Abe took his finger away from his lips, looked at Shia, and took a heavy breath.

"Do you think she needs to respond?" Abe asked.

Silence filled the room. James had called it a suffocating silence, Tic-Tac remembered. When the silence started to settle over the open spaces, no one could take a breath. Shia didn't answer; he followed Rachel's lead and cast his eyes down, unwilling to challenge Abe.

Kelsey continued her questions with the expectation that Rachel would nod or shake her head. Yes or no responses disguised the absence of tangible answers. These trials in the committee had become a witch-hunt, where Kelsey pointed fingers at treachery and refused to hear the replies. To her, all signs pointed to a person being a witch, even if no signs existed to begin with, Tic-Tac thought. She cited absent cans from the pantry, missing pots and pans, footprints to and from the woods as proof of these kids helping the outliers. All the false accusations and the committee's attempted persuasions of each kid were enough to make Tic-Tac dig his nails deeper into his hand, causing the warm trickle of blood to run along the lines on his palms and coagulate beneath his fingernails.

"Don't we need a witness?" Tic-Tac asked. He couldn't watch anymore; the line of questioning felt more pathetic than investigatory. He couldn't watch Rachel tremble in the small space she filled. Her clothes looked empty, absent of mass.

"We have one." Kelsey's voice was shrill and brazen, the opposite of Abe's dry and calm tone, but filled with the same venom.

"Let's just have them come and say something," Tic-Tac said.

"We don't need that," Abe said.

"What's that supposed to mean?"

Abe looked at Tic-Tac, but there was something lacking from his stare. Tic-Tac had once found playfulness in Abe's eyes. Now when Tic-Tac looked into Abe's eyes he saw emptiness.

"The witness told me in private, out of fear of retribution. I will respect their privacy and we in turn will punish the rule breaker," Abe said. He pressed his finger back to his mouth and tapped at the small imprint at the center of his upper lip. He looked back to Rachel. She finally looked away from the floor.

"I think we've heard enough. Stockade till you admit you broke the rules or until you tell us who did."

Two boys came from the darkness and started to take Rachel away. She kicked and threw her arms.

"You can't do this!" she screamed. The boys dragged her out of the committee.

"I told her she'd know when it was her turn to speak."

"Shouldn't we know who the witness is too?" Tic-Tac asked. "We're all on the committee together. You can share the information with us without the person fearing retaliation."

"No," Abe said. "They told me in confidence and I'd hate to betray their trust."

"What about the rest of our trust?"

Tic-Tac felt everyone's eyes on him in the flicker of candlelight.

"What's that supposed to mean?" Kelsey asked.

Abe put his hand up and Kelsey stopped talking. His black fingertip festered.

"I'm sure there's a valid meaning," Abe said. "Isn't there?"

"I just meant . . . " Tic-Tac looked to the window and swore he saw the shadow of the Icedome creeping over the settlement. "I just think we should know too."

The cold used to stop at the door; lately the chill came through the cracks of every crevice imaginable. It didn't matter where Tic-Tac was—the dining hall, the committee, in his room tucked up in bed for the night—the cold crept up and down his skin, especially when Abe gave him that lifeless stare.

"I'm just trying to follow the rules," Tic-Tac said.

"The rules have changed," Abe said. He turned and walked out of the room, whispering something to Kelsey as they left together. She laughed. Andrew came and left the meetings with his usual silence. He hadn't said a word since his appointment to the committee, *and he probably never will*, Tic-Tac thought. The committee was a game and Abe had stacked the odds in his favor for when they called a vote. Abe was right, the rules had changed, and *he* had changed them.

"I'm scared about this," Shia whispered. He hadn't stopped staring at the table. Rachel's shrill screams continued in the square.

"What?" Tic-Tac asked.

"Nothing," Shia said. "I didn't say anything." He put on his coat and left the room.

It had been two days since Rachel's trial. She had been tied to the beam for two days. Two times a day someone came to give her food and wrap her in a blanket for a few hours, mostly at night when the temperature dropped severely. Tic-Tac came into the stale shadows and wrapped Rachel in a coat and gloves. She slept with her knees snug in the ground, her arms dangling above her head. Her forehead pressed tight against the wooden beam. The gray daylight layered the sky surrounding the settlement. Sarah slept in their room, unaware of Tic-Tac's absence, he believed.

"Please," Rachel said.

Tic-Tac kept walking. In San Diego, when he would see a busker on the street with a sign that said something like "Homeless, need help" or "God bless," he avoided eye contact and kept walking. In the square, he kept his eyes on the flickering light of the room in the short distance. When he reached the door on the far side of the square, he wrapped his fingers around the handle.

"I didn't do anything. I swear," Rachel said.

"I know," he said. "But that doesn't matter now." There was an extreme pain in his chest he tried to ignore. Inside the room, he couldn't escape the image of Rachel's frozen hair dangling around her face like spikes.

A KNOWN
HIDING PLACE

JAMES

THE CRUISE SHIP WAS HOLLOWED OUT BY COLD AIR AND empty space. Flames had licked and charred the insides. James and Charlotte found shelter in what had brought them to the island. He exited the trees with an empty bow and an otherwise empty hand, failing at hitting his target. There were enough deer on the island to keep James and Charlotte full.

James held the bow and arrow in his hands and looked at the sharp tip at the end of the shaft. He couldn't help but think of Geoff's wrinkled face blurred beneath a layer of blood. James didn't want to think about the sharp arrow tip, but more so the sharp tip of the knife Abe had wrapped James's fingers around before he plunged it into Geoff's chest. James was never much of a hunter. The deer had stood in James's sight, grazing at the deep-rooted weed that poked through the ground. The deer dug around the weed and pulled at the snow. She breathed gruffly, her snorts visible in the air. She tapped her hooves on the solid ground and broke into the soil before continuing to dig. James watched with passionate curiosity. The hole the deer dug became deep and wide. The deer placed her face into the hole and reached for plant roots.

The echo of dogs was absent from the day. When James pulled the arrow back, the deer looked up with wide eyes and twitching ears. It probably didn't see him. That didn't matter. When it was just James and Charlotte, she understood when he couldn't let the arrow loose.

"You'll get it back," she said after she had shot their first deer, second deer, fifth deer. But after three months had passed, they were not the only ones hiding in the burnt-out cruise ship, and James could not afford to stay the arrow any longer. James's face was no longer smeared with blood. A healed scar stretched over his left cheek just beneath his hair. He hadn't cut his hair since before he entered the Icedome, and it was now long and coarse.

"I like it," Charlotte said, running her fingers across his forehead.

"I just . . . " James said. "I don't know. It gets in the way."

"Of what?" Charlotte asked.

"I don't know," he said. His hair kept him warm now that they lacked the settlement's heating system.

James walked back to the ship empty-handed. Many of the rooms were lost in the blaze, molding into one open space that was accessible through the hole in what had once been the engine room. They had stripped the ship bare before it ever erupted, but James often hoped he would stumble upon some hidden mattress, piping, blanket, or pantry no one had seen. He hadn't yet.

"You still can't?" Charlotte asked with a look of exasperation. Her cheeks had sunken in the previous weeks. Her hair was as stringy as his. They didn't wash often, and for a while, the stench of their bodies had made them both want to retch. It had been some time since they dealt with the overwhelming reek of body odor. With time they became used to it. However, as new kids wandered from the settlement, it was easy to say they had followed their noses, true or not. "You have to deal with it. We can't go on without a hunt anymore."

Charlotte stayed back to look after the ship, which had become a new settlement across the island from the old one. They hoped they could live in some semblance of solitude and security beneath the radar. But what had begun with just James and Charlotte soon became James, Charlotte, and Sarah. The next week, three more people arrived.

It couldn't have been a coincidence. The rumor of James's survival must have started sometime after James and Charlotte left, and once the rumor started, it wasn't likely to be forgotten.

"I didn't ask for—"

"I know," Charlotte said with a heavy sigh. "Neither of us asked for them but they're here and we need to address it. We can't keep going on like it's just you and me. They're looking to us now and we said we would come back with food."

"You should have gone," James said. "I can't—"

"I couldn't. Today was the run." Charlotte's tired tone disappeared, lifted suddenly into a smile. "We did pretty good."

She continued to reach into the sack beside her, lifting out cans of food filled with green beans, pulped tomatoes, and carrots. James remembered once taking those same cans out of the ship's pantry.

"They still have cans?" James asked. "I thought they would be long gone by now."

"Apparently they have stocks," Charlotte said.

34

"Abe locked them up shortly after we left. I thought it was because they had more vegetables from the greenhouse or something but . . . "

"How'd you get them all here?"

"I think he's just not letting people eat," Charlotte said. She looked into the small fire that flickered beside her. "I think the only good thing that came from your fight in the dome is that you're not afraid of the ice anymore."

They tried to keep their supplies limited. If they left little evidence of their existence, they might go unnoticed. It was all they could to do to keep the unwanted gaze of the settlement off of them. One advantage of having only two people in the cruise ship was that the wood lasted longer. James ended up chopping wood more often than he thought he needed to; it was a job he soon handed off to someone else. The longer they stayed, the more it seemed everyone at the settlement knew the outliers were there. They should just chop down all of the goddamned trees so they could stay warm like the goddamned settlement did with their god-damned thermal heating.

"You didn't even stop the first time," Charlotte said. "When we came that night, you could barely walk."

"I was more afraid of the dogs," James said. "I thought they would jump us the moment we stepped into the forest."

"But they didn't."

"No, they didn't. Then I thought they would get us when we walked out of the forest. I had this elaborate plan to fall to the side, drag you with me, and let the dog—or dogs—smash into the ice. Obviously we didn't need that plan." James coughed—a violent reminder of the time he fell into freezing water.

"They look sallow," Charlotte said.

"The dogs?"

The fire fizzled. Charlotte stopped digging into the bag for more cans.

"The kids in the other camp. They look too thin."

"Have you seen yourself lately?"

"We haven't exactly had the benefit of a mirror."

Her hair had gotten long based upon where the old white dye dipped past her chest. The brown in her hair was more prominent, coming down to her ears, followed by a long stretch of snow-colored hair tainted with grease.

"How did you get these cans here?" James asked with concern. They weren't supposed to be seen; they weren't supposed to exist now. They had wanted the settlement to believe they had wandered into the woods and fallen victim to dogs or cold. James never wanted Charlotte to go on a run in the first place, but she had convinced him. They hadn't had enough food; they hadn't had enough warmth. At the time he barely had enough life left to breathe.

"I'm going to the settlement," she had said.

"You can't," he mumbled through a handful of ice pressed over his face. His cheeks were bruised, his eyes were swollen, and not all the blood had been washed off his face after days of attempted rest.

"The deer won't help and we need more blankets. We need more everything."

James reached for Charlotte's hand in the dim light of the cruise ship. She grabbed his hand and lifted his glove until they could see his pale skin. She pressed her warm lips to his wrist. "I'll be right back," she whispered. She did come back hours later as James shivered in the darkness, riling with what-ifs. She had a sack filled with two blankets, two cans of sugary fruit mixture, and three cans of mixed vegetables, along with one extra coat with a broken zipper.

"Apparently they were throwing this stuff away," she said.

"How?" was all James managed to say. Charlotte lit another small fire.

"Ingenuity," she said. That night she cooked an entire portion of mixed vegetables by shoving the can directly on the fire. "No one will know. I promise." Someone must have taken notice eventually. After a few weeks, when Charlotte went on a run, the take became bigger. After what felt like a few months, James grew stronger. He offered to go on the run.

"You can't get caught," Charlotte said. "It's too dangerous."

"So I'm left to hunt and let you go alone?"

"One," she said, "I'm the better hunter. Two, it's more dangerous for you than for me. Three, you wouldn't know what to do."

"It's not safe for you either."

"More than it is for you."

That was the end of the conversation. Charlotte continued to make runs when they ran low on food. James's nightmares continued whenever he aimed his bow at a deer that stood close enough for them to have for dinner.

Now they were alone in the dying light of the fire. Charlotte looked back at the stacks of food she emptied from the bag.

"How did you get all of that here?" James asked. It was too much to carry on her own. Someone could have seen her. She could have left too much evidence behind. Had she left a trail from dragging the sack through the woods?

"You should take one of the new kids with you next time you go hunting," Charlotte said. "They may—as in, they would—have more success than you."

"Charlotte!" he snapped. She looked at him with vibrant eyes that looked larger than when he'd first met her.

"Sarah went with me."

Charlotte had stacked the cans in a pyramid to measure her success. James wanted to knock them all over, take them back to the settlement, or bury them beneath the ice. He felt the cough rise in his lungs but tried to suppress it. It only made it burn more.

"She wanted to see Tic-Tac. She missed him and I needed someone to help me carry it all back," Charlotte said.

"Is that how you came out with so much each

time?" James asked. "You can't do that. This is too much. They'll notice! Abe will notice."

"I don't think anyone will notice, not anymore."

James knocked over the pyramid. They survived only by the grace of Abe. He must know Charlotte and James were holed up in the cruise ship, but he didn't pursue them. *Why didn't he take us months ago?* James wondered.

"We have to take some of this back," James said.

"We can't," Charlotte said. "You don't think I knew it was too much? You don't think I told Tic-Tac we couldn't take all of this? He wouldn't take it back. Whether he was giving it to Sarah or not, it's ours now. You haven't seen what that place is like. They won't notice."

"I'm worried they already have."

"Something's wrong," Charlotte said. "Haven't you noticed more kids pouring through the woods, risking dogs and ice? From what I've overheard, they're more afraid of getting caught trying to leave."

"So were we," James said. "That's nothing new." They couldn't hold more kids whether they came for safety or sanctuary; they could barely fend for themselves. James couldn't tell if the world was getting colder. He had felt a terrible chill running up and down his spine since he left Geoff stone cold with a knife in his chest.

"It's not the same," Charlotte said. "It never will be."

SOUNDS
OF A BREAK
JAMES

JAMES MISSED MUSIC THE MOST. HE COUNTED HIS FOOTSTEPS like drum beats, using the snowy crunch as symbols whenever he needed a clash. The beats to songs he used to sing swam around his memory without words. On starless nights the thoughts of a guitar, the way the strings sounded when someone strummed them all at once, rattled his teeth. Even if the notes he remembered, strung together like a clothesline, weren't the same songs he once heard, they kept him going.

Abe never cared about the sounds of humanity, James thought. Music scared Abe because it brought people together. Except for when he and James had broken into the record store. Abe had searched for connection that night, a reminder of what it felt like when his parents were around, James knew. Music had the power of nostalgia, ambient sorrow, and happiness all at the same time. Abe never felt connected to the world, maybe. *And now he thinks he owns it.*

James stomped hard on the ground. Sometimes he would forget where he was and pound a tree with his open fists. Frost would shimmer down from the leaves onto the ground.

"Is it getting warmer?" Charlotte asked in their hideout inside the ship.

The small fire crackled. James tried to add unremembered words to a song. He tumbled around words like "sheer-hearted magenta" and "fruit-tree poisoned youth," but couldn't hold them together in his head any better than he could a snowflake in his hand before it melted from the contact.

"Did you feel it?" Charlotte asked. "There's just something during the day that doesn't seem to feel as relentless as before. I thought you would have noticed."

"Why would I have noticed?" James asked.

"You have frost on your shoulders," Charlotte said. She held onto a pathetic smile, one she couldn't see, one she may have not known she wore. He was too aware of the faces she made as he grasped at the music all too absent from their lives.

James never realized how much he missed music until he sat in the absence of it. When he was stuck in the cell after Geoff died—no . . . after he killed Geoff—he listened to the soft wisps of steam and tried to make songs out of the gentle wind instrument, making incoherent sentences that sometimes fell out of his mouth when he wasn't paying attention.

A few days ago he had been hunting with a group of new outliers. Cheryl and Phil had been part of the hunting group in the settlement, two of the best. Cheryl wore her brown hair short, which became the trend after they mastered the heat and didn't need to worry about the cold inside anymore. She probably regretted the decision now that she didn't have the warmth of the settlement. Phil wore his dark hair long, a trend for most of the boys after the snow fell that had yet to change. They had all fallen into complacency, not wanting to change the routine of their lives that had been uprooted so often. When life started to work out for everyone, James didn't want to adjust any part of his routine, choosing instead to wake up every day at the same time, eat the same breakfast, and wear his hair the same way. He drew the line at wearing the same clothes all day, every day. Clothing changed, it was an inevitability. But James realized change would come whether he altered his routine or not. Come hell or frozen water, the world kept turning, according to the shifting light of day.

James joined the hunt because he needed a job to do. Sitting around the ship with nothing to do would have felt worse than his failed attempts to shoot deer. He had become adept at tracking, but whenever he came close to a deer it would hear him step.

The damn music in my head scared the prey away,
James thought.

Sometimes he would get close enough to the
thoughtful figure to stretch the bow back, ready
to let loose. Did he breathe too loud, or could
they hear the fibrous flick of the bow string as it
stretched? It all came to the same outcome: the deer
would look up, twitch its ears, he'd stay quiet, hold
his breath, and eventually the deer would catch a
whiff or sound of James and flee.

That morning, Charlotte had to convince James
to go with Cheryl and Phil.

"It's a bad idea," James said. "They're two people
Abe will notice are gone."

"You don't think he hasn't noticed anyone else is
missing?" Charlotte asked. "We weren't that big of a
place to begin with."

"It started to get bigger."

"Have you seen any kids around here? It's not
from lack of trying. We can't take kids here, they'd
never survive."

"We did," James said.

"And we will," Charlotte said, "as long as you get your butt out there and learn to hunt. It'll be fine."

Cheryl, Phil, and James set out into the forest. As they came to the tree line, James looked up toward the sky in search of the ever-present smoke. It became a tradition along the lines of a superstition, a beacon to anchor him to the island. The smoke sifted through the sky that continued to look like cobwebs.

He followed Cheryl and Phil. The bow and arrow rested while James tracked. They came across hoof prints in the snow. They found pulled weeds and broken branches, along with a freshly dug hole.

"I once had a deer at my tea party," Cheryl said.

"I had never seen a deer until the island," James said.

"I saw some at the zoo once," Phil said. "It was Christmas and they had reindeer walking around a pen. The whole place was lit up with blue lights." Phil took sharp cold breaths through his words.

Cheryl was quiet. James swallowed hard and held his breath every eight steps to contain his cough. At one point he pressed his hand to the tree and doubled over, every molecule of oxygen burning in his lungs when he took a breath.

"It's shocking you were never able to catch a deer," Cheryl said.

"I caught one," James said.

"Rumor has it Charlotte caught that deer," Phil said.

"Can't argue with a rumor," James said.

They wound their way through the trees. The canopy blanketed the sky. Sporadic light broke through the leaves. Cheryl, Phil, and James walked in different rhythms. Cheryl chipped at random tree bark to mark their path; Phil would sometimes kneel to the ground and dip his fingers in the snow. He never wiped them off or sucked the cold from his fingertips afterward. He would stand up and walk like he hadn't taken the time to touch the snow at all.

"What was that?" James asked Cheryl after the third time.

"He's superstitious," she said.

"Aren't we all?" James asked.

"He's checking to make sure we haven't wandered off onto the ice; something like that."

"Wouldn't the trees tell us that?" James asked.

"Not always," Phil said.

He moved to the front of the group. James had thought they would have spotted a deer earlier, as if by having Phil and Cheryl with him, the deer would have appeared by magic. So far all they found were broken branches, a few tracks, and a constipated rhythm.

The beat rumbled in James's head again, whether from boredom or inspiration, an irresistible thump of the music he wished he could emulate. He started to rap his fingers against his thigh where space was left between his glove and his pants, a small movement he thought would go unnoticed. He fingered the air like piano keys. The snow chomped louder.

The imagined strums of a guitar plowed through a musical sky rumbling beneath the canopy.

James smacked his hands against his thigh. He felt the tingle in his skin, a distant ache that began to reverberate around the padding of his pants—hit, smack, thwack, hit—until he gave up the noise, opened his palms, and slapped at the nearest tree with raw heat. The tree shook, its leaves waving the most they probably had since it was covered in ice. He kept slapping at the trunk imitating the noise in his head without success, without caution, without regard for the people around. He had forgotten there was anyone else there at all.

Cheryl put her hand on James's shoulder. He stiffened—stopped. His breath was harsh. He felt he could never catch it. She pressed down harder on his body. He wanted to push her away. He hated the way her hand felt on him. She had to press hard or he might not feel her touch from underneath the layers of clothes. He missed being touched. Like music, he took for granted the simple feeling of someone's skin on his skin, where even in the cold, a simple touch could warm him. The heat wouldn't leave his body now; it was stuck on his cheeks as he tried to fill his lungs with fresh air that didn't come fast enough.

"Lucky there weren't any deer anyway," Phil said.

"Maybe we should head back," Cheryl said.

"We should—" James said. A low howl tore through the trees. James was an awful hunter and a worse shot, a terrible drummer, and was on the verge of becoming paralyzed by superstitions, but he had learned the sound of dogs. The first howl carried across the sky, then another, and another. The first moan was high and long, from a single dog. The second roar was lower, a short burst from a different mutt. The third wail came as a myriad of animalistic clamor, encompassing the entire pack in a single burst. Cheryl, Phil, and James stood quiet. The pressure of Cheryl's earlier grasp shifted from endearment to fear.

"If we stay quiet," Phil said.

"If they're as close as they sound, they'll find us by our scent," Cheryl said.

James sniffed himself. The heat from his musical outburst surrounded him. He wanted to strip down and press his body into the snow. He hadn't felt this warm since he first stepped onto the cruise ship and was wrapped in the warmth of central heat. He took off his beanie and looked at it. He hadn't looked at his clothes in a long time, himself in an even longer time. Had the dimensions of his face changed like Charlotte's? When her face started to slightly hollow, her eyes grew bigger. Every time she looked at him lately, with those large green eyes, he tried to slip into her stare and remember a world covered in lush plants instead of ice.

His beanie was frayed at the rim, the gray knit splitting. He turned the hat over and over in his hands, looking for the front or the back of the circle. Threads struck out from the rest of the hat, reaching for freedom, freedom from suffocation beneath the weight of other threads. Why was it so hot? When was the last time he took his beanie off? When was the last time he touched his hair with his actual hands, not the gloves, but with his crispy, cracked fingertips running through his unwashed mess of hair?

James howled. He ran the beanie over and over again around his hands and howled a second time. The dogs howled back in the distance. He couldn't tell if they were closer or farther, less or more.

"What the shit are you doing?" Cheryl asked. She grabbed him and started to pull him. This wasn't fear or empathy, it was the harsh twist of anger that dug through the layers of his clothes. He howled again.

"You're going to get us killed!" Cheryl said.

He dropped his beanie to the ground. He needed air and he needed to cool off. He needed to take off his coat. He reached for the zipper and felt some air swoop through his opened jacket. The dogs' howls grew richer, a chorus of winter creatures reaching out to the three of them.

"We need to go," Phil said.

"Obviously," Cheryl said.

"They're going to help us," James said. "It's getting warmer." James wiggled his shoulder and tried to take off his coat, but Cheryl's hand guided him forward, keeping his coat on. "It's too goddamn hot!"

"What is he doing?" Phil asked.

"How the hell should I know?" Cheryl responded.

The howls moved closer in the shadowed light. James didn't want to dance anymore. He wanted to dive beneath the ice. He needed to cool down and the snow was the only way. It sounded so refreshing now, but once seemed to scare him more than anything.

He moved through the trees, pushed by a buoyant touch that urged him forward but kept him from taking off his clothes. The trees all looked the same to him. The light shifted from bright to glaring. The beams searched for him between the leaves.

"They're right behind us," Phil said. "We need to run."

"We can't run," Cheryl said. "He can't run."

James howled again and the dogs returned his

song. The wind blew against his face. It was cold on his cheeks. His legs carried him faster through it. The trees brushed by him, turning the world abstract.

"You have to push him," Phil said.

"I don't know how long I can," Cheryl said.

"We don't have time to switch."

James stretched his arms out into the wind. Cool air flowed into the jacket sleeves and around his waist. He tried to lift his shirt but couldn't get it past his stomach. Too much time, too much effort, too much heat, not enough air, the sounds of the dogs carried him away from the burden of his memories.

"The tree line," Cheryl said.

"They don't come past the tree line?" Phil asked.

"They won't go on the ice."

The fresh air flew past James faster as he found himself hugging the slick ice, with short, wheezing breaths. His eyes closed. Howls loosened in the distance. Cries for help broke through the silent, gentle balance of body heat and cold air he held onto.

THE BETRAYAL
OF US

ABE

STALE AIR HUNG IN THE NIGHT. ABE SAT IN THE WARM darkness of the committee, waiting for someone to enter the room. People were leaving the settlement. James and Charlotte had survived, he knew it, and they must have known he knew it, but Abe wanted them to live. A part of him hoped one day they would come back to the settlement and serve out their sentences. They could mold back into this world they had helped create. They could help protect the settlement's future, making it possible to survive the endless winter. People ran to the opposite side of the island and Abe couldn't figure out why, but he knew they wouldn't survive for long.

He had woken up in a cold sweat beneath the spearheaded shadows of forgotten trees. The dream of Elise's knife recurred, washed and clean, set on Abe's bedside table—a trophy shimmering in the non-existent daylight. A gold plate etched on the stand exclaimed, "The source of power!" Abe knew immediately what it had meant; it was the knife Abe should have taken James's life with. Except Abe had tossed the knife into the graveyard. It was supposed to rid his mind of imagined ghosts and real shame.

The more Abe had the dream, the more he smelled the metallic scent of death coming. The dream had told Abe one thing: James and Charlotte were alive. Abe's heart played tug-of-war with itself, hoping James both lived and died. Abe wanted to grab the knife, Elise's knife, from his dream, and shove it into James's chest. The whole purpose for leaving San Diego in the first place was that they had wanted to live. Why did that feel so impossible?

Abe wiped the sweat from his forehead. An overwhelming feeling of nausea washed over him. What happened to them that they couldn't even keep the settlement together? Ever since Elise died, the settlement had gone crazy. Abe wished he could go back to the days when it all fit into place like a fractured but functioning puzzle. Some pieces were bent or torn, but they still knew how everything fit together. Now it seemed they weren't even using pieces from the same box.

The door opened and Tic-Tac stepped inside the committee. The soft glow of the candle hit the right side of Abe's face.

"I was wondering if you would come," Abe said.

"It's really weird that you're sitting in the dark," Tic-Tac said.

"I don't like to waste things," Abe said. "There's no need for more than one candle."

"How can you see anything?"

"Your eyes will adjust. Sit."

Tic-Tac made his way slowly to his chair, the one he took during committee meetings. He sat in the quiet flicker of the candle and made no noise, not even a scrape of the chair on the floor.

"I know you don't like Kelsey," Abe said.

"Who said I don't like—"

"Cut the shit. It's me and you, this isn't a committee and I'm not going to run out of here and *tell on you*."

Tic-Tac gave a nonchalant smile that said he didn't care. In the half-light of the candle, Tic-Tac looked tired. His eye had a slight twitch Abe had never noticed before. Tic-Tac used to be a dreamer, filled with some belief it would all be okay no matter what happened. It was obvious the way he used to stare at James while he read fantastical stories with happy endings. That look was absent from Tic-Tac now, the gentle glow in his eyes and the quiet upturned corner of his lips. In the simmering candlelight, Abe thought Tic-Tac looked more like a man, but no matter how Abe looked at anyone, including himself, it was hard to see past the childhood they never had.

"Why should I hide my dislike?" Tic-Tac asked.

"You don't need to," Abe said. "In truth, I'm glad you don't. Your honesty is important."

"Then I think she shouldn't be on the committee

at all. She doesn't have the knowledge or the experience to help anyone."

"We didn't either, once," Abe said.

"But we do now. So do others." Tic-Tac let his arm rest on the table and started to tap his fingers quietly against the metal. "I think you chose her because she sides with you."

"I didn't know she would do that when I chose her," Abe said.

"You didn't?"

"Of course not. I chose her because she wanted to learn and we need more people to take that step from out there to in here."

"This isn't a school. We don't teach in here."

The harsh tone in Tic-Tac's voice came through. The controlled force behind his words told Abe he had been holding onto these thoughts for a while.

"Why didn't you say anything sooner?" Abe asked.

"Because people—I didn't want to cause any problems."

Abe knew Tic-Tac lied, because he looked straight at Abe, as if he had to force himself to look into Abe's eyes to convince Abe, or himself, that what he said was true. After so long in Fornland, and long enough on the island, Abe thought he knew people well enough to figure out how they hid themselves from the world. Tic-Tac did it with force. It was obvious when Tic-Tac lost his faith in the happy endings. Abe had noticed Tic-Tac falter in his connections to other kids, to Sarah. Tic-Tac left them aside, pretending he protected them from his crumbling insides, when it was really himself he was trying to protect. Tic-Tac told his truths in a way that would make him feel better: he stared directly into a person's eyes. The harder he stared, the more the person believed him. Tic-Tac overpowered the person with his eyes. He did that now, except Abe wouldn't accept it the way others had.

"What were you going to say?" Abe asked.

"I said what I meant," Tic-Tac said.

"If you said what you meant you wouldn't have had to stop saying it."

A heavy quiet grew between them, stuffed with anticipation. He knew what Tic-Tac had to say but waited for him to say it. Seconds passed. A minute. Two minutes. "People are afraid of me." Abe gave into the quiet. He once thought speaking first showed weakness. In a battle of snow versus ice, sometimes one had to give an inch to gain a yard.

Tic-Tac hesitated. "Yes."

"Why didn't you say that?" Abe asked. "You afraid too?"

"No." Tic-Tac kept his stare, first for seconds, then a minute. Tic-Tac was scared of Abe too; Abe now knew.

"Good," Abe said. "I need your honesty."

"Then you'll have my honesty."

Abe and Tic-Tac both kept their jackets on. Sweat trickled down their cheeks. Abe thought it added a second layer to their battle of wills, the willingness to be uncomfortable in the presence of another.

"More stuff has been taken from the stocks," Abe said.

"I'm aware," Tic-Tac said.

"I figured you would be."

Tic-Tac continued to silently tap his fingers against the table. "We need to stop this from happening."

"To stop it?"

"I have done everything I can think of to discourage this act of rebellion. Maybe it's time to take care of the outliers."

"You know about the outliers," Tic-Tac said.

"It wasn't hard, especially when people started disappearing. I don't know how they'll survive out there. I just want them to come back and be safe. There's only a certain number of people that can survive on their own."

Tic-Tac tilted his head, a slight but noticeable movement. Abe watched every finger tap and lip-curl as they spoke. Tic-tac's involuntary flick of his head showed he knew more than he let on. If he didn't know where the outliers were, he at least knew why people left. His lies would prove useful one way or another.

"How do you suppose we do that?" Tic-Tac asked.

"I think we need to find a more definitive way to cut off their supplier." Abe moved closer to Tic-Tac in the warm, dark room. The space closed between them as he leaned closer still. "Do you have any idea who could be giving them supplies?"

"No," Tic-Tac said. "If I knew I would tell you. I don't like what's going on any more than you do." Tic-Tac didn't let his look linger. He turned towards his tapping fingers, now stalled in midair. "Sarah's out there too, you know."

"I do," Abe said. "I want to bring her back to safety."

"What about the rest of them? What about James and Charlotte?"

"There is no reason why we can't coexist. They just need to serve out their sentences and be done with it. We can move on . . . like it never happened. Can you figure out who it is?"

Little was left of their world before the island, even less of a world of friendship and family. Abe wanted his best friend back. He wanted his girlfriend back, but when all was said and done, he knew the latter was gone forever. If his dream said anything, perhaps any chance for a world of friendships had died too.

"I can," Tic-Tac said. "But you have to stop."

"Stop?"

"What you did to Rachel." Tic-Tac's voice rose as if he questioned whether or not Abe remembered who Rachel was and how he had punished her.

Abe covered his face. How could he explain to Tic-Tac, to anyone . . . to everyone, all he wanted was to keep everyone safe? Abe had to show people why the rules were important. If they couldn't see it, then people would run all over the settlement and their civilization would break down.

u're scaring people away, Abe. You're scaring
ryone."

"Not you?" Abe asked.

"Everyone else," Tic-Tac said.

"We need to stick together."

"We all do. We all need to understand." Tic-Tac looked straight into Abe's eyes and didn't lift his gaze from the flickering light that kept Abe's pupils wide. Abe had been sure of Tic-Tac's tell, or at least his need to feel superior. Now Abe wasn't sure. Tic-Tac was on Abe's side, though; that was all Abe needed.

"You'll find out who it is?" Abe asked.

"I'll find out."

Tic-Tac stood up to leave. Abe stared into the dying candle where the wax pooled beneath the flame. Soon the puddled wax would snuff out the light it had cradled.

"I'm glad you're still here," Abe said. "You're the only one left who understands."

Tic-Tac sighed loud enough to fill the room. Abe kept watching the flame.

"I don't think anyone does," Tic-Tac said, walked out.

True silence didn't exist in anything less than darkness. Maybe Tic-Tac was right and no one understood. Maybe all the understanding went the day Elise died, the day they made it to the island, the day they left San Diego, the day his parents died, the day he was born. Maybe the world was filled with misunderstanding the way the night was filled with stars and the ground was filled with snow, and no one, anywhere, would ever understand him again.

UNDER A CANOPY
OF SHADOWS

CHARLOTTE

THE ISLAND WAS FROZEN AND DRY. THE COLOR OF NIGHT wasn't enough to hide the dim flicker of windows that let Charlotte know it was safe to call out from behind the trees.

She had left James behind; he couldn't have come if he wanted to. The fever had taken over his body, and he was pulsing with sweat and blush—a ripe strawberry ready to burst. She missed her strawberry vines in the greenhouse. The glass windows reflected small light and she wanted to step inside to visit her old plants, to surround herself with a verdant aroma, rustic potatoes, and sweet fuchsia. Life wasn't some fantastic journey, a coloring book that took them through the world together, marking each city and country they visited with a vibrant blue or green, rather than the all-encompassing white that smothered the world in freezer burn. Charlotte hadn't seen a paper book in ages, let alone a coloring book. She fashioned a bed made of stolen blankets and left James covered, stripping him down and laying more blankets over him.

He had spent the first night shivering while she pressed ice to his forehead. *Snow shouldn't melt that fast when someone touches it,* she thought, otherwise Charlotte would have palmed the snow over every inch of the island just to get a glimpse of the ground below. When she touched James he stopped giving into the impulse to tremble; she stripped down and pressed her body to his beneath the blankets. She brushed her sweaty hands over his greasy hair. His heat kept her warm. His eyes were closed; he probably didn't know she was there, didn't know she held him, touched him, caressed him, that he warmed her in the disturbing cold. She needed him in her life because she needed someone to keep her going, to tether her to this crusted earth, something to look forward to every day. Elise had lost that and Charlotte would be out of luck if she couldn't wake up every day and find a reason: the greenhouse, Autry, James, anything she could help that in turn helped her. It was part of the routine: open your eyes, get the fire started, make breakfast, find a project, fix something, cook food, hunt, stoke the fire, search the island, listen to the dogs in the distance, stare at the mountain as little as possible, stoke the fire, cook more food, go on a run, guide people to the outlier, stoke the fire—don't let the fire go out.

The settlement was quiet. Charlotte examined the angles of a particular bush. The branches needed to be placed in a way that looked natural to passersby, but unnatural enough for Charlotte to notice they had changed. She had to wait, and waiting led to more thoughts she didn't want. She contemplated what her life would have been like if James hadn't let Elise leave the kitchen with that stupid knife. They all could have been cozy in the settlement, James standing in front of everyone with a story on his mind and their attention on him, some tale about the earth's humble beginnings or why the sky danced, even though the Northern Lights had disappeared some time ago. It wasn't a seasonal phenomenon; how had they disappeared after Elise died? As if she were the reflection of all the light left on earth, now all the night sifted through the excess light to create nothing more than distant lifeless starlight, or worse, the tormenting light of a full moon in the dark.

Charlotte stood behind the tree and waited, hidden from the smattering of kids who came and went through the square. She kept herself from yelling out to Autry as the little girl stepped from the greenhouse, apparently having taken over the responsibilities of growing food in Charlotte's absence. Charlotte would know Autry even bundled up like a marshmallow, from the dangling hair that came out from under Autry's beanie, to the way she walked with her hands clasped together with some-thing tight in her fists, like hope, unwilling to let go. But Charlotte pressed her lips to the tree bark instead, unable to call out, keeping herself hidden in the forest like a secret everyone already knew.

"It's too soon," Tic-Tac said. "You were here a few days ago. They'll find out."

"Don't act like they don't already know," Charlotte said.

"I meant about me," he said. He leaned against another tree hidden in the shadows from the lights beyond. He looked older . . . not older, but sadder. It had become the same thing. Slight wrinkles formed around his eyes and mouth, soft enough to be hidden from most people but detailed enough for Charlotte to see them.

"I need medicine," she said.

"You look fine," he said. "I'm sure you don't need any—"

"It's for James . . . "

Tic-Tac stood straight. It wasn't enough to have

pulled James from the water; there was a draw to James Abe had never seen. Tic-Tac was too much of a hero to not help, even when he made it sound as though he couldn't. James never thought of himself as a hero, she knew, but he saved more lives than he would ever know. He had saved all of them. *Or at least he tried,* Charlotte thought. Before they had left the settlement, Charlotte heard children cry; some people would get annoyed with the whimpers and tears, but Charlotte listened with a fast heart and wet cheeks. It was a reminder that their life continued, that they survived and she had helped. They followed James straight to the end of the world and he never even knew it.

"What's happened to him?"

"He's sick. He has a fever. He won't make it."

"If you thought it was tough before . . . we're on lockdown when it comes to most stuff. I can't get medicine out of here, especially now. You heard what they did to Rachel."

"What makes you say that?"

"You'll have to figure out another way."

"How's Autry?" Charlotte looked to the green-house as if Autry would be there, hands clasped together, locking the door behind her.

"Scared," Tic-Tac said. "Everyone is."

"Why hasn't he come for us?" Charlotte asked.

"He knows where you are but he just lets it go; he keeps saying that our food is running low."

"That's what all the new kids say. They tell me that's what urged them to leave in the first place; food couldn't keep them here anymore because you were almost out."

"Except we're not. There's so much left. But not medicine. There's a limit."

"You think I don't know that? I wouldn't ask—"

"Unless you really needed it. Right."

A distant howl made Charlotte uncomfortable. She heard James make those noises when he passed out on the ice, face down, arms splayed open. He had a big grin that made Charlotte want to leave him there in peace; if it had been another day, one where Phil and Cheryl hadn't come to her, frantic about dogs and James going nutty, she may have let him lay there in that awkward afternoon, breathing in the icy dust. Even in his sleep he howled, grin slapped on him, naked beneath the blanket, close to Charlotte without any knowledge of how he felt when she kissed his neck and said "I love you," words she hadn't said since her parents died to anyone other than her stuffed walrus, Franklin.

"While I'm here I might as well get some food too."

"Of course," Tic-Tac said. He rolled his eyes. "Tell me how she is."

"You saw her a few weeks ago," Charlotte said. She could see her breath sit between them with each word.

"These days a lot can change in an hour, let alone a few weeks."

"Sarah's fine. She misses you. She wanted to come but I—"

"Good, she shouldn't come. It's too dangerous."

"You boys say that far too often. You think we can't take of ourselves?"

"I don't want to be the reason she gets caught."

"You wouldn't be. She'd be the reason because she wants to see you, not because you want her to come. Boys are kind of stupid."

"I'm beginning to realize that," Tic-Tac said. The distant howl broke up their conversation, followed by a clamor of pots from the kitchen.

"They check every dishwasher now. Makes everyone nervous. I need to go soon."

"I know," she said.

"No," he said. "I need to go with you."

"Soon, hopefully, you won't have to."

Tic-Tac stepped back into the small light of the settlement. Charlotte stayed behind the tree and waited for his call when he set the bag of food and medicine aside. The first time she came, she worried more about wild dogs than the repercussions. The more she made the trek, the more she felt comfortable with the wild and less comfortable with what would happen if she were caught. Dreams of standing in the dome with a plank of wood tied to her back while Abe drove his fists into her stomach and cracked her face replaced the nightmares of her parents' death. When Abe started to punish people he thought were helping the outliers, Charlotte wanted to give herself up to protect anyone else who might be next . . . but she wanted to survive more.

The far bushes rustled. It was the sign the bag was in place. She counted to five hundred and checked the area. She went to grab the bag. She looked inside and waded through cans of vegetables and fruit cocktail, along with fresh apples. How many times was she told not to accept open goods from strangers on Halloween? Stories of candied apples filled with razorblades had spilled out of her mom, and now Charlotte had to almost beg for them, wishing they were covered in chocolate or sugar. She kept pushing cans and fruit aside, looking deeper until her entire head was inside in search of the medicine. At the bottom she found a black sock; she assumed it was dirty but she could never tell with black socks. In the sock was a small collection of white pills, around ten, enough to help James get through the worst of it. Once again the evening sky filled with something more pressing than her worry about the dogs—the possibility of losing her boiling boyfriend to some sickness that could have been beaten by a bowl of chicken soup.

"Are you taking us?" a weak voice asked. It belonged to Daron. She had spent the last months of Charlotte's time in the settlement making deodorant. This wasn't the first time Tic-Tac hid refugees with the food. Charlotte couldn't turn her back on them, not after what she had seen, heard, thought, dreamed—not when all anyone wanted these days was to turn back the clock to before they feared more than just the cold.

Charlotte's nightmares of her parents' car crash continued to haunt her. The less comfortable and more occupied her mind, the more meager the nightmares. It was a positive in a frozen sea of negatives. Everyone wanted to turn back the days, but no one would ever agree upon the distance, leaving them all to wallow in an assortment of misery, just not their current struggles. She never told James she led packs of people to the boat; she kept the secret to protect herself because she knew James wasn't wrong about new faces and the dwindling score of the settlement, because of Tic-Tac, because of her.

"Tonight is—" Charlotte said.

"Please," Daron said. "We can't be here anymore." Two other faces Charlotte didn't recognize nodded along.

"Be fast, be quiet, and just follow." Charlotte took the bag and turned into the forest.

"We're going in there?" It was a boy's voice, as weak as Daron's but filled with fear.

"There's no other way to go."

"There're dogs in there," he said.

"Take your chances one way or the other." Charlotte grabbed Daron's hand. "Hold tight and close." Daron grabbed the boy's hand who grabbed the final girl's hand and they crept through the closed forest together under the canopy's shadow.

WISHING WELL

CHARLOTTE

THE GROUND OUTSIDE THE SHIP WAS BARE AND WHITE. Charlotte's footprints marked the soft snow with dim pockets. The night was quiet all around the ship, from the silent stars to the nervous kids who had started to fill up the empty and blown-out compartments once again, like old times, for the few months that everything seemed perfect. From a distance, the ship looked frozen in mid-sink. A large hole opened along the starboard hull. The hole made the labyrinth of halls and doorways vulnerable to the elements. The lobby was stark and coated with smoke stains. The halls tilted. The ship wasn't the lively home they had once shared, no matter how much Charlotte pretended.

81

Charlotte came into the room to find James lying next to the fire, his bare shoulders open to the flame that puffed. Someone kept the fire going while she was gone. She needed to remember to thank whoever it was later. She needed to feed James the medicine Tic-Tac had given her. James hadn't eaten anything in days. He was too tired, too sick, to even open his mouth. Charlotte came close to shoving soup down his throat the other day; the frustration overwhelmed her. How could she want to help someone who was too sick to help himself, too sick to know what they needed? James couldn't give up and neither would she.

Charlotte lifted him up and let his open back hit the frigid air, away from the fire. She had the medicine in her hand and tried to force the pills in his mouth. She hoped they would work. After time aboard the ship and away from doctors, she didn't know what sickness he had—whether he held a bad cold, a slight flu, or something worse. Whatever it was, she hoped it could be cured with simple medicine; that was all the island had. She pushed the pills to James's lips. His eyes stayed shut. The flicker of the fireplace shone on his face. His cheeks glistened with sweat, absent of acknowledgement. Did he notice her at all anymore?

His weight was almost too much to bear as she tried her hardest to keep him steady and feed him the pill at the same time. He swayed and wobbled, falling back and forth. She kept him steady long enough to push the pills to his lips. She watched them stick to his tongue and not go any further. He needed to swallow them. Why wouldn't he swallow?

"Take the pills James," she said. Her voice was softer than the fire. "Take the pills and we can get rid of this. You can come back to us . . . to me. You need to come back."

She saw the pill stuck to his tongue just beyond his slightly parted lips. It hadn't budged and it wouldn't disintegrate. He would swallow water. The cup by the fire was filled with melted snow. She tried to reach for the cup without dropping James. It was a balancing act in a circus of which she never wanted to be a part. His body stood against her knee. Her hand reached for the cup, grazed her fingers just out of reach. She had to extend her fingers a little more, but the more her body leaned, the more James dipped back to the ground. She had gone on the run and didn't have the energy to lift him back up once he fell; her body ached from her fingers to her toes. She attempted one last quick swoop of the cup. She leaned toward the fire but pushed too far. She fell away from James. James fell to the floor. The cup was in her hand but James was on his back, eyes closed, lips parted, unaware of the difficulty of simple things.

Charlotte saw Franklin by the fire and grabbed him. She needed the comfort of home, which faded more and more from her mind. The memories became dreams, and dreams had the ability to drift away once she woke up. Franklin's fur was soft, his mustache fuzzy. A walrus could easily survive in a frozen climate. Once taken away from its home, a branch will crack and wither. Charlotte felt that way now more than ever, having fallen from the tree long ago, thinking she was strong enough. The longer she hid from the settlement, the more James looked like he would slip deeper into sickness and the more she felt like she had shrunken from a branch to a twig, unable to fight the waves and the ocean, ready for the world to snap her. In those moments, her body chilled, filled with pain and overworked. She couldn't even sit by the fire with her head in her hands and cry. She held onto Franklin instead, filled with the unspoken fear that if she could cry the tears would freeze to her cheeks.

"Do you need some help?" Sarah asked. She stood by the hollowed-out door with her purple mittens dangling around her neck.

"Why aren't you wearing those?" Charlotte asked.

"Sometimes it's just better to let my fingers breathe." Sarah walked into the room close to James's feet but with her back close to the fire.

"He needs medicine but I can't get him to swallow. I can't hold him up." She loosened her grip on Franklin and slowly put him down.

"I'll hold him," Sarah said. "You give him the water."

Sarah lifted James's upper half from the floor and Charlotte spilled drops of water into his mouth to wash down the pills, making sure none of the water dripped down his chin and his chest, onto the blankets below. He swallowed the pills; Charlotte could see his neck twitch with every shallow gulp of water. Sarah laid James on his back and Charlotte covered him back up with the blanket.

"I saw some new faces tonight," Sarah said.

"This place is a hot commodity," Charlotte said.

"Won't be long, I suppose."

"Until Tic-Tac joins the exodus?"

"No," Sarah said. "Until Abe decides to come looking for us." Sarah stared into the fire with a face absent of concern. Her face looked absent altogether, no emotion one way or the other.

"What makes you think he'll come at all?"

"You know him better than I do and I know he won't let this go on for much longer. We're all shocked he turned his head and let so many of us leave. What was he like before?"

"You knew him before," Charlotte said.

"No," Sarah said. "No one really did, but everyone wanted to."

"I didn't really either," Charlotte said.

"Do you think Tic-Tac will be okay?" Sarah looked at Charlotte; her eyes gave way to the fear Charlotte hadn't seen earlier. Sarah may have left Tic-Tac behind but not because she wanted to; it was written on her face. She did what she thought she had to do—*as we all keep telling ourselves.*

"He's worried about you too," Charlotte said.

"Why didn't you take me with you tonight?"

"I didn't take anyone with me tonight. It was too dangerous."

"Too soon after the last run?"

"Among other things. He wants to join us soon. I don't know if that would be a good idea or not, but he's looking bad."

"He's hanging on," Sarah said.

"Sounds like a lot of people we know," Charlotte said. She looked back at James. How often had the world picked them up and lifted their spirits only to drop them again? When would they tell the world they weren't going anywhere? If they hadn't left by now . . .

Sarah stood up and brushed off whatever stray remnants of snow or ash or sadness may have clung to her. "It'll be over soon."

"I'm worried about what that means," Charlotte said.

"A lot of us are." Sarah walked out of the room. The shuffle of her small feet gave way to the sporadic crackle of the fire. Charlotte pressed her ear to James's lips to make sure he breathed. They all had lost enough in their lifetime; she wasn't willing to give up anything else—not to the cold, not to the world, not to Abe. She would hold on.

FOLLOWING
A DIFFERENT LEAD

ABE

THE DARKNESS SEEMED TO AGREE WITH THE QUIET. ABE wasn't sure which had come first, but for some reason they went together nicely. He took a sharp breath in the cold night. He inhaled the frigid air that encircled his body. The cold would either spread over the warm parts of his insides and freeze, or soften. So far the latter happened over and over again.

The stars were absent; the Northern Lights were absent; the moon was absent. On a night like tonight, the darkness took over and spread across more than the sky, leaving shadows in the distance or a flicker of a dying candle somewhere in a window. Abe sat in the greenhouse and looked out to the tree line. It wasn't hard to make out the distinct shadows of the trees that formed the dark wall in the distance. Kids had made their way through that wall for weeks now, disappearing into the silhouette and leaving forever. For a while, Abe thought the dog howls were signs of content— that the feral animals were fed and happy with the supple meat of children, calling to the empty sky in a form of homage or warning, and letting the settlement know that anyone who wandered into the woods would follow the lost bodies of those that came before. It was the image the committee tried to portray as well. No one had known that James and Charlotte made it out of the woods. Abe tried to convince himself he didn't care, but the more he tried to ignore that feeling of hope, the more it festered inside him. Not the hope James had been attacked by the sharp vicious teeth of the rampant dog pack, but the hope that James had made it through to someplace safe. It was an icy mixture—this incompatible combination that forced together Abe's abrasions: whether he wanted his best friend to live or die and whether they could be called best friends at all anymore.

Abe looked over the covered portion of the window in the darkness. He knew no one could see him but he hid in the shadow of the glass anyhow. The room smelled of herbs and fruit. He wouldn't take a banana even if he were hungry; that would be against the rules and if anyone broke the rules it wouldn't be him. He tapped the window and traced his finger over the frosty glass in the same design he traced on his sheets, cut into his bread, and had carved into his door: Æ.

When the night started to shape Abe's eyes, he sat in the darkness more and faded out the light. He no longer wanted to be a fireman, but someone who worked in the dark—some sinister thing that worked in the dark, more than a shadow. Shadows are attached to the light; they are formed, shaped, and contorted by the light. Abe craved the absence of light and spent more time in the committee and his bedroom watching the darkness wrap around the night, while everyone else snuffed out their candles and presumably laid their heads on their pillows until morning. Sometimes Abe saw the moon casting billowy figures sprawling from the trees, but it turned out to be the trees themselves. The jungle harbored the howls of feral dogs. What was darker than the night itself? What could look into the darkness and see the shapes it covered? *Nothing but the night*, Abe thought. As he traced his finger over Æ again and again, he whispered in bursts of smoke, "Be like the night. Be like the night. Be like the night. Be like the night."

In the silence, a darker shadow moved toward the tree line. The open space between the greenhouse and the jungle spread into a no-man's land that showed every step a person made. The silence did the same, crashing the soft snow in the air like a cymbal. Put them together and the clues formed a picture: someone snuck away from the settlement thinking the dark would cover their tracks. When would they all learn that tracks couldn't be covered in the snow?

Abe left the greenhouse's humidity and walked into the open. He closed the door tight to make sure the air wouldn't seep out. His methodical tendencies came with all his time away from San Diego. With every touch of every door he thought about how much heat he could let seep out of a building or how much cold he could let fill a different room. He made sure the door couldn't be opened by a gust of wind.

He followed the silhouette sinking behind trees and listened to the footsteps echo beneath the canopy like a symphony played for him. The cold-needle smell of spruce wafted from the frozen leaves and bark. If Tic-Tac wouldn't find the person responsible for stealing food and guiding people out of the settlement, Abe would. This must be the person. No one else would be ballsy enough or dumb enough to step out into dog-infested woods alone in the dark.

Abe traced the letters onto his wrist as he marched through the trees, creating an invisible shield. The howls didn't scare him; the darkness was another color he fit into, more than the morning gray and the icy blue. The comfortable dark rushed around him and let him see the light clearer than he had ever seen it before.

"I will find you," he said in a whisper. He couldn't see his breath as he pushed through the snow, following the crash of footsteps. "The darkness won't protect you."

The trees loomed like guardians, protecting a secret Abe needed to know. He came across the lanky figure. The silhouette spread from the bark. The shadow whispered to nothing. It hunched at the shoulders and swayed. The harder Abe looked the less he saw, until the shadow split in two, and a taller figure arched over a shorter one.

"Come back with me." Abe heard the words

bounce off of the bark with a drum beat but couldn't find the shadow from which the noise came. "I don't want to be alone anymore." Both silhouettes could have shared the words. The words could have been taken from Abe. He tried to come closer to the two; some magnetism he couldn't escape drew him closer to them, as if they would understand him because of how they pushed one another away but wanted desperately to return.

"Something's there," the taller shadow said. It was a man, as much of a man as anyone on the island could have been.

"Someone or something?" That came from the smaller of the two, a woman, a soft voice, not scared but curious, a voice not afraid of ghosts or darkness.

Abe didn't move; he waited for their anxiety to dissipate. He wished he could slip into the nothing and get closer to hear what their whispered secrets were before his steps gave him away. As he waited for the quiet to soothe the two shadows, he heard a sound. It wasn't a person but a collection of shuffling feet—or paws—along the tree stumps. The steps gained speed.

"We need to get out of here," the taller form said. "That way," and the two shapes flew away as the sound began to rush closer from the direction Abe had come.

Abe took off after the shadows. The pack of steps came closer, no longer a cymbal or a drum, now just a boom of snow pounding against the ground. A howl rose through the trees. Abe thought he saw a light in the distance, a burst of color on the back of a parka, possibly blue, with a fur-lined hood. Tic-Tac. It had to be Tic-Tac running with someone up ahead, someone he didn't want to be without anymore—Sarah. The howl came closer and mixed with the booming snow. Abe's breath came slow. He was ready to burst. His legs ached from toe to thigh. He couldn't catch his breath, suck in air. He fell down—the dogs came closer.

"Help!" Abe said. "Tic-Tac?!" He reached into

the emptiness to arms he couldn't see and hoped someone would find him before the dogs did. No matter how much he had hoped, he realized now he wasn't like the night. The dogs ran closer in the darkness. The night was almost over and no one was around to grab his hands and pull him to safety.

THE UNBEARABLE PRESSURE OF A GIFT

CHARLOTTE

IN THE CRACKLING CONFINES OF THE FIRE, CHARLOTTE HEARD the rushed and dragging footsteps of people who marched through the hallway with hushed voices. The fire sizzled late in the overbearing darkness with a tiny glint of color. She hadn't rolled beneath the blankets with James yet. Some part of her urged her against it, told her to stay wrapped up in her own arms, near the flames. She should let James rest on his own. The physical distance could assert an emotional distance as well, an ever-present draw to plan for the worst. The worst wouldn't happen today or tomorrow or the day after; James would get better, sit up on his own, swallow the pills on his own, and give some reassurance to everyone who had fled from the settlement to the semi-frozen ship that bordered the frozen world.

The voices outside her room came closer with the unmistakable dragging of feet over cold ground. The halls wound through the ship's interior but the windows from each room had either been poached or blown out. Holes riddled the ship, which allowed the frigid air and flakes to get through.

"She'll probably be asleep," a male voice said.

"We need to wake her," a female voice said. They continued to step and drag, step and drag. Charlotte wasn't sure how many people were outside her door and if what they dragged was a part of the group or a separate . . . thing. No one ever needed to wake her after a hunt. If they brought back an animal, they had a steady protocol: take it to where the kitchen used to be. The cavernous space contained some elements of kitchen-ness left that made it fine for the hard work of draining deer, skinning them, and cooking them—all of the steps they needed to maintain in order to not starve, freeze, or find themselves swimming in an over-burdened state of drool dripping from their faces and freezing around their waists.

"I'm not asleep," Charlotte said. She looked over the fire that had kept burning since the day James had made it, when they first came to the ship and his ribs were battered. She would never forget the purple and green mound that wrapped over his side when she tried to help him through the jungle. He winced and ached; his arm had wrapped around her but each step felt labored, not just to him but to her, as he dipped and dragged his feet, his toes in particular scraping the icy surface of the island. She couldn't forget that sound halfway between life and death, filled with the unbearable pain that James had tried to hide by holding his breath and telling her he was fine. The longer they walked, the shorter his breaths grew and the more he relied on her. She didn't expect him to move when they got to the ship but he had insisted on getting wood and starting the fire. James never stopped fighting; he couldn't stop fighting. He wouldn't stop now.

The voices entered. It was Tic-Tac and Sarah, holding a third person between them—the source of the drudging sound. It was Abe. He looked asleep or passed out, limp between Tic-Tac's lanky frame and Sarah's daintiness.

"What is he doing here?"

"He followed me into the jungle," Tic-Tac said. "I think."

"Put him down," she said. The two laid him down close to the fire. "Not there. You find something to tie him to and put him in the corner, away from the fire." Her hands shook and wouldn't stop. A tremor formed in her voice. She wondered if Tic-Tac and Sarah noticed. If they did, they hadn't said anything. It wasn't from fear; it was from anger. Charlotte had spent the past months, what may have even added up to over a year now, thinking how Abe could have led them all to a safe and beautiful existence on the island—existence, not life. Living wasn't what anyone did anymore; they existed—survived. If they were lucky enough they would find moments of comfort floating by, giving them enough rest from whatever they needed to escape from, a reminder of why they pushed forward at all. The comfort refreshed them enough before the struggle began all over again, until that next wave of salvation draped over them for a brief moment. Charlotte was convinced that that had finally caused Elise to snap. She had never felt that wave or relief and couldn't fathom moving on at all.

Tic-Tac and Sarah bound Abe's hands and feet and laid him in the corner facing the wall, as Charlotte had instructed them to do.

"Did he see you?" Charlotte asked.

"I think he did," Sarah said.

"I'm pretty sure," Tic-Tac said.

"Think?" Charlotte said. "Pretty sure? You two need to know. Did he see you or not?" Charlotte stood up and walked over to them. She put her hand on her own shoulder, desperate for any form of consolation, a yearned-for hug. She could feel her chest squeeze against her heart. The faster it moved, the harder it was to see Tic-Tac and Sarah in the dim light of her room. James hadn't stirred. Charlotte stepped closer to the pain, ignored her pacing heart, and put her hand on Tic-Tac's shoulder. "It's more important that he didn't see you than her. Did he see you?"

"He did," Tic-Tac said. "He called my name."

"What happened?" Charlotte said.

"Last night I left the ship," Sarah said. "I had to get a message to Tic-Tac."

"You had to?" Charlotte asked.

"I needed to see him," Sarah said.

"And you put us all in danger for it."

"I didn't know if he'd even show up."

"I didn't know anyone had seen me," Tic-Tac said. "It's my fault. I found out after, when it was too late."

"Yeah," Charlotte said. "It's way too late." She shot Sarah a look of disappointment. Charlotte imagined it was the same look her mother had given her a lifetime ago. Charlotte's mother had sat at the kitchen table with an exam paper in her hands. A circle surrounded a large, red *F*. Her mother ticked her tongue and stared at the page. The window frame above the sink framed her face. The sadness in her face was harder to stomach than any anger Charlotte's mother could have shared.

"I just know you're better than that," her mom had said. "I don't understand why you didn't try your best. I'm not mad. I'm just disappointed."

Shame rumbled in Charlotte's stomach at the time. It had been a stupid test, one that hadn't even affected her overall grade in the class. Her mother's simple, calm tone pierced Charlotte's skin. Why hadn't she tried harder? The simple phrase followed her around. A stupid exam started to matter, and Charlotte had to try harder from then on, always worried that if she didn't try harder then she would disappoint her mother again. She refused to fall short of her potential ever again, unwanting—unwilling—to feel less than her best.

But Charlotte understood Sarah's desperation, and in a way, her separation anxiety, the need to help when weighed down by helplessness. She wasn't angry with Sarah; she was disappointed by Sarah's carelessness, her selfishness. It was the same look Charlotte's mother had given her, she knew.

In the dry cold of the cruise ship Tic-Tac said, "There were dogs."

"We thought we could outrun them," Sarah said. "We did but we're not sure if Abe did or not."

"Why didn't you leave him there?" Charlotte asked. She looked past the two into the corner where Abe laid hogtied, going nowhere.

"You're joking," Sarah said. "Right?"

"Tic-Tac," Charlotte said. "You need to go back to the settlement now. Sarah will show you the easiest way."

"You weren't serious," Sarah said. "About leaving Abe there?"

"No," Charlotte said. "I wish I had been. I think I need some air. I'll walk out with you both."

The difference between Abe and Charlotte, Abe and James, Abe and anyone sitting in the frigid ship instead of somewhere warm in the settlement houses, was that they clung to an idea, one which took them away from their possible comfortable existence—the idea that Abe had changed into a deceptive animal, manipulative and crazed, unwilling to compromise, unwilling to listen, unwilling to let them all live. The conclusion they made: you were like Abe or you weren't, another simple black-and-white, a place where they drew the line so definitively that Charlotte could see the divider in place, demarcating the specific moment when the shadows became evil and the light became good. If they had let Abe slip into the dogs' mouths, life would have been easier on all of them, but it would have stepped over the line to which had they were drawn and clung.

"You both did the right thing." They walked through the labyrinthine halls of the ship that were streaked with soot, endless chunky reminders of the explosion. They hadn't found any bones; somehow that comforted Charlotte in the maelstrom. Burnt-up wallpaper and crusted stucco opened in gargantuan holes to burnt-up wiring and hollows.

"What are we going to do?" Sarah asked. "Maybe we should have left him there." She looked to Charlotte and then to the floor as if she punished herself for the thought. "I needed to see him, Charlotte. I—"

"It was my fault," Tic-Tac said. "I wanted to—"

"It was nobody's fault," Charlotte said. "Neither of you could have known, and the truth is, it could have been worse. You weren't bringing food and you weren't going on a run. I think it'll blow over."

"But now he knows where you are," Tic-Tac said.

"He already knew. I'm sure. We're going to have to figure something out, sooner rather than later." If Abe hadn't known, which was unlikely, he would know when he woke up. The hair on the back of Charlotte's neck stood as chills ran down her spine. Abe would wake up and she would have to figure out what to do with him. If James were awake, he could decide what should be done with Abe, whether they all moved back to the settlement and let Abe go free or they let Abe die. The thought felt like icicles poking at her from head to toe. If James were awake he would decide whether Abe lived or died so she wouldn't have to. She wouldn't have to bloody her hands. She took off her gloves and stared at her palms as if the sanguine fluid had already stained her skin.

PIECES OF LIFE

SARAH

THE SKY CONTAINED A SMATTERING OF LIGHT IN THE DIS-
tance that Sarah made out as one blurred line
over an icy expanse. She led Tic-Tac to the settlement even after he protested that he knew the way.
"I don't want you to have to walk back alone," he
had said.

"Maybe I won't walk back at all," she said. The
bright spark of hope glimmered in his eye and gave
her more joy than she remembered having since they
first got together. That glint in his eye made her
hope that the statement could be more than a *maybe*
and turn into truth.

"I remember that look," she said.

"What look?" he asked.

"You used to look up at James that way when he read."

"I remember. I know."

"There was that look again, just now, when I told you I might stay—that same hopeful look. I think that is what was missing from you."

"The look, I know."

"No," Sarah said. "Hope."

"It's overrated, I think," Tic-Tac said. He swatted at leaves and branches for no reason; they weren't in the way.

"Because you were able to live without it for so long?" she asked. "I have known you before and after . . . " Her voice trailed off in a way she didn't mean, letting the words scatter among the trees. Her throat tickled in a way that told her she didn't want to let the words go—not out to him or in the forest; she preferred to hold onto them. No matter what people said, words could hurt and the last thing she wanted was to hurt Tic-Tac.

"I didn't hear that last part," he said.

"Because I didn't say it."

"I haven't always been hopeful." He swatted at another branch. The light stalled in the distance. No matter how far they walked, it wouldn't rise. It was like a cartoon where they chased the distance in circles while the landscape never changed. She hadn't thought about cartoons in a long time. Cartoons didn't matter anymore. Why would she think about things that didn't matter? Cartoons had been filled with joy, a joyful experience meant to make people laugh—children laugh. They mattered more now than she had ever realized—at least the laughter did.

"I remember your laugh," Sarah said.

"Why do you have to remember it?" Tic-Tac asked. "It hasn't gone anywhere."

"Yes," Sarah said. "It has. Do you remember the last time you laughed?"

"Not off the top of my head." Sarah said nothing. They came to the edge of the settlement. What was worse: not remembering the last time he laughed, or not noticing that it had been that long? They were one in the same. His laugh was a full-body experience; it wasn't jolly or timid. She would watch it start in his stomach, a little jolt before his shoulders sputtered. He would shake his fingers as if the joy pricked his fingertips and he had to fling it away. The sound was what she enjoyed the most, a full, present gasp of air, more than a wheeze but less than a yell, a sound she couldn't pinpoint but could recognize from anywhere in slow deep bursts, as he threw his head back, eyes closed, ecstatic.

Her hand wrapped around his, her fingers within centimeters of his skin but not touching, distanced by layered gloves that kept out the cold but simultaneously kept them from each other in the smallest ways. She could break through his visible breath and kiss him while they stood on the border of the settlement that separated them, a selfless separation on his end but selfish on hers. She never had to leave but she chose not to be around who Abe had become. Charlotte had been sneaking onto the grounds for weeks and needed help. Sarah had been Charlotte's contact and grabbed what she could when she could. If Sarah left, no one would have been around to help Charlotte if she and James needed food or blankets. A few kids started out on their own, hoping to find James and Charlotte. They came half-starved, half-dehydrated, and fully defeated. Sarah guided them to Charlotte sporadically until Sarah told Tic-Tac to stay because she couldn't anymore, and he did because he was loyal—more loyal than she had been when she left without him.

Abe now lay in a corner in the ship. Sarah could stay with Tic-Tac, at least for the day. The pressure of the invisible line that divided what the settlement meant from what the ship meant was palpable, almost oppressive. Tic-Tac took a step; his step could break down the wall that Sarah couldn't see, but felt. He pulled Sarah's hand with him, not noticing she didn't follow. Again, she would leave instead of sticking by the person she had broken through the woods and the midnight to visit.

"I should get back," she said.

"You said you'd stay," he said.

"It's almost day." She nodded into the horizon blocked by the jungle, a horizon they couldn't see until they reached the exposed ice beyond the canopy. But she didn't pay attention to the trees and the sunlight. Why didn't she just go with him? She wanted to be with him.

"Abe won't be here. At least not today. Not until they figure out what to do with him. Come inside. We can get warm." He drew at her arm once more; again she didn't move. She couldn't take the step over the threshold. The warmth almost seduced her. At some point in the past weeks the warmth had tainted her. Heat was only found in the settlement. Staying in the settlement meant she had to pretend, but at least she'd be warm. Warmth meant that she gave up the ability to choose, fight, run, help, disagree—gave up the right to be herself. She would instead be stuffed with fear, a staple of a routine that kept her mouth shut and eyes cast down.

"I can't," she said. "The dogs are gone. I should go."

"They're never gone, you know," Tic-Tac said. "They eat, sleep, shit, and hunt like we do. They're never gone."

Sarah took her hand away and held onto it. Any hand was a source of comfort in the wasteland of the day. Tic-Tac's eyes lost that shine where hope once stood. His face turned back into a sunken rubber band, elastic in how it shifted from hopeful to hopeless in a matter of words—those words that people once said couldn't hurt, that differed from sticks and stones; if sticks and stones can break her bones than words could truly kill her.

"I know you're right," she said. "They're never gone, even when you think they might be." She didn't wait to hear his response or whether he had one at all. The snow shifted beneath her feet as she turned and ran toward the light that she hoped waited at the other end of the jungle.

EYES BURNT WIDE

ABE

A GENTLE SILENCE MIXED WITH THE ABSENCE OF FIRE. ABE knew that the smoke rose and the darkness filtered through the air which had once been bright. He couldn't move his hands or his legs; they were bound tight by coarse hairs that rubbed against his wrists. Whoever tied him up knew how to tie a rope tight and that it needed to touch his skin, otherwise he'd be able to wiggle out by taking off his clothes, one piece at a time. He searched for an answer to where he may be. He noticed the harshness of the air, the lack of any heat; he lay next to a wall. He knew he was in the bowels of the ship.

This new world he was crammed into smelled of

shit and yellow snow. The acidic pungency made him want to sneeze, while the putrid fragrance of actual, collected shit made him gag. Where did that smell come from? He gagged again and searched his body for torn clothing, blood, pain that came from something other than the searing pain in his shoulders, ankles, and wrists. Somehow he had made it out of the jungle alive without a scratch from the dogs. He could've sworn they almost had him, nipped at his heels. *Guess you're not right all the time.* Was there a way out of the room, a way he could make it back to the settlement without being seen? Seen . . . who had he seen walking through the trees in the middle of the night? Maybe they were still in the room, asleep in the cavernous vacancy where a fire once was. He turned his head and body away from the corner. He rolled and twisted to see if he could remove his limbs from the tangle. He writhed like a slug covered in salt; when was the last time he had seen a slug? As much as the bubble and sizzle of a salted slug amused some of the kids he had grown up with, he never enjoyed that display of "strength." Now more than ever, he sympathized with at least part of the slug's endeavor to live. A memory of Elise's face lifted in the light of the room, smeared with the faint sharp scent of shit beneath a blanket, beyond the flame that was no longer stirring.

"You know what that smell is?" the blanket asked. Abe didn't respond. He knew the voice. He could pick that voice out of a loop of uninterrupted sounds. James sat huddled beneath the blanket. "I know you know what the smell is."

Abe knew the voice but it lacked the acuity of James's normal tone. It was small and raspy, like muffled sandpaper—like orphaned snowflakes. Abe's eyes adjusted to the slight difference of light between the room's darkness and the darkness behind his eyelids. James's face was sunken, cheeks drawn back toward his mouth. His fingers were bone from a distance, the flesh torn away as the scaly hands held the blanket over his shoulders. From under the gravelly voice poured a skeletal James.

Beneath the tepid warmth of the blanket, Abe saw the look of death emanating from his best friend— or at least who his best friend once was.

"Where's it coming from?" Abe asked.

"There's nowhere else to go. The ship is half here, half blown to hell. We can't go out there, on the ice, to the trees. People have been choosing rooms. Luckily it isn't hot. You remember how shit smells in the heat?"

"Like twelve miles of overflowing intestines wrapped up in a dead man's rotted chest," Abe said. "Why am I here?"

"Beats the goddamn out of me," James said. He pulled the blanket tighter around his shoulders and shivered. "I woke up, the fire was gone, and you were stuffed in the corner like a prize deer."

"Want to untie me?" Abe asked. The strain in his own voice ached throughout his body when he spoke, from his pulled-back head to his ass. He tried to keep his talking to a minimum to not hurt as much, but something pulled at Abe that made him want to simultaneously say every word he knew and say nothing at all.

"No," James said. "I really don't."

Abe couldn't see James's eyes, tucked somewhere in the shadows beneath the blanket of an already dark room and screened by wisps of smoke.

"Why haven't you come for the ship yet?" James asked.

"I didn't know you were here," Abe said.

"Bullshit. You knew. It wasn't hard to figure out. Where else would we have gone?"

"Maybe you found another hot spring. Could you untie me?"

"No. Stop lying." His voice exploded with hatred and betrayal. Abe didn't blame him. He couldn't. He held James close and made him press the knife into Geoff's heart. Those were the rules. One winner, one life. James needed to do it and Abe helped him. That was what they had founded the settlement on: rules.

"They were rules, Hamez."

"You don't get to call me that anymore."

"We need to follow the rules."

"Fuck the rules! Where did they get any of us before? We still ended up in a goddamned boardinghouse, stuck on a cruise ship, floundering on a frozen island. Elise is dead—"

"You don't get to talk about her." Abe couldn't scream; the breath caught in his lungs got stuck somewhere around his constricted ribs. Someone needed to untie him. Why did they bother saving him from the dogs if they were going to store him in a burnt-out room anyway?

"You're the only one who gets to say her name? She was my friend too."

"And you let her go. I guess that's what your friendship is," Abe said.

"That's a hell of a thing to say."

"Just come back and serve out the punishment. You don't have to live like this."

"How's that?"

"Just surviving."

"That's all we've ever done." James coughed and spit blood into the stack of burnt tinder. Abe had trouble breathing at all now. His wrists were chafed and his body started to tingle with pins and needles from the troublesome blood flow. *Bite into the silence, be like the dark,* Abe thought. There were numerous ways Abe thought he could make it past a moment like this, but he looked over at James, or the thing that James had become, and all he wanted was his friend.

"Please," Abe said. "Untie me."

"You remember when we were kids and we let that dog into the fortune cookie factory?" James asked.

Abe nodded. He had opened the back door. The next thing they knew there was a series of crashes and shouts from the workers inside.

"No one working there was Chinese," James said. "You were so disappointed, like it would have given you some sort of answer to the universe."

They watched through the window as the dog

ran around the factory eating all it could, chased by a series of guys, some overweight, all of them Hispanic, running after a shaggy, black mutt that left hair in its place.

"That dog could eat. And fast," James said.

"We followed," Abe said and gasped. James coughed again.

"It followed us around for the next hour before it started shitting out fortunes. Remember? His turds looked like they had chunks of sprinkles in them and then a single strand of paper stood out."

"I wanted—"

"You wanted to read them. I never figured out why. But you followed that dog around the rest of the day. What was that fortune you got?"

"Happiness . . . " The sear became an ache that became a pound on his rib cage, chest plate, rattling his bones.

"Happiness will be yours," James said. "I've thought about that a lot."

The room started to disappear, replaced by

dots, black dots that came and went whenever Abe blinked. He made it through dogs to die this way. He made it out of San Diego to suffocate from an inability to move his arms and legs. *What a world,* he thought. *What a world.*

He closed his eyes and his arms and legs flew apart. He took a gasp of cold air and choked for a brief second. The blood rushing through his body was more painful than when it couldn't make it to his toes and hands. He rolled onto his back and took another breath. He balled his fingers into fists. The tip of his index finger remained black, with a hint of green.

At night in the empty space of his room, Abe swore he smelled rot emanating from his fingertip. He opened his eyes. James knelt over him, naked except for the layers of blankets wrapped around him. He nudged his shoulder closer to Abe. A tinge of pain swelled around his balls.

"You know what that is?" James asked.

A splintered arrow tip edged into Abe's crotch.

James held the arrow firm, eyes fierce, ready to shove the arrowhead into Abe's scrotum, Abe realized.

"I thought you weren't ready to kill," Abe said. "I thought you were better than that."

"Maybe you won't die. But you can be damn well sure that if you move in a manner I don't like you'll bleed out in an incredibly painful way. Your call on how this ends."

"Come back, serve out your time."

"I can't do that. We can't do that." James loosened his grip on the arrow. The tinge of rugged rock moved away from Abe's skin.

"This how it ends?" Abe asked.

"This time," James said. "Just go."

"I'll have to come back," Abe said. "Don't make me come back." Abe stood up. His body felt as unstable as a sack of snow.

"You already made your choice," James said. "Now I have."

James couldn't kill Abe and Abe almost pitied him for it. James didn't have what it took to lead.

Abe sat there defenseless, tied up, and James released him. Abe didn't pity James; James was just pitiful. Mercy was foolish and deadly.

"Don't make me do this," Abe said.

"You don't get it, Abe. You chose this. This is on you."

Gray light rose over the island. Abe made his way back to the settlement. People were out, moving toward their chores, ready for a hunt, walking to the greenhouse, the smell of breakfast still lingering. Had no one noticed him missing? They created this world; how could no one have noticed him not at breakfast or in his room, not around? What did James mean Abe had chosen this? This world was thrown on him as it was on James. He didn't choose this. *How could anyone choose this?* Abe would rather return to San Diego and take up surfing, commanding the waves rather than fearing the ice. The closest he wanted to be to ice was sipping a cold drink on a hot day. No one should have chosen this life. Except James had. And that would be the last choice he ever made.

EMPTINESS
OF ANGER

CHARLOTTE

CHARLOTTE WALKED BACK INTO THE ROOM FILLED WITH THE emotive glances of misunderstanding, not knowing why the room looked more vacuous than when she had left. Fire turned to smoke and drifted over the rustic wood that no longer flamed. There was nobody in the corner, another absence that worried her. She couldn't forgive her indecision and complaint from minutes earlier when she had wanted Abe's image to go away, fade to black, disappear—die. Now that he had, a bad feeling lingered in his absence.

Since the snow started to overtake the world, she filled herself with an undeniable remoteness colder than the actual air, and when she saw a fire, part of her wanted to jump into it. Elise used to run to the block-fires when the snow started, when buildings erupted like fireworks and what felt like the entire underside of the city showed up to warm their hands. Now that the fire in the room turned to ash, it filled her mouth. The lack of warmth, even from a simmering light, was dry and unwanted. The flakes turned to an inescapable soggy crust.

Over the adverse twigs, James wasn't there. Two bodies that had lain lifeless in the room now both disappeared, apparitions that left Charlotte wondering if it had all been a terrible dream to begin with. Maybe she never made it out of the settlement; maybe James never fought with Geoff, perhaps Captain never died, maybe snow never drifted over the landscape at all; maybe she would wake up in a bed with her parents down the stairs, a fire in the fireplace, Franklin, her stuffed walrus, sleeping next to her comfortably, ready to bring in the day. It was a flashback that allowed her to see that she shouldn't be scared, shouldn't run, wouldn't run, but could find James just the same if she wanted to. A new rush of wind came through the door and wrapped against her visible cheeks. She felt them turn from red to pink to ice. She did the normal thing when someone questioned whether they were asleep or awake—she pinched herself, hard, on her wrist beneath where her glove met her sleeve. Franklin sat by the empty fire; his whiskers billowed in the breeze.

When she was young, Franklin spoke with her father's voice. Franklin hadn't spoken in years. Even if he had, she couldn't tell her father's voice from a sharp wind. After her parents' car crash, she had ignored the possible soft tones or harsh yells because she missed them too much. After a while their voices turned into strangers. She would rather forget her parents altogether than border the likes of strangers. She had to take off her other glove and let her fingers squeeze in the sliver of skin that she showed, pale. A quick, slight, hard pinch and the pain ran up her arm. It wasn't a dream.

If she wasn't dreaming, where was James?

He stumbled in from a different corner away from where his body had been. His feet straggled, his body wrapped in a contortion of blankets. He was awake. He stepped closer to where the fire once burned and dropped down along the empty pile of clothes that remained. Franklin didn't budge. She almost ran to James, tackled him down to the floor in some effervescent display of emotion that almost overcame her. She could show her happiness, her elation that he was okay. Why did she continue to hold it back? By not letting James know how relieved she was, it would help her in case he relapsed, or Abe . . .

"You look better," she said. She walked over to James and sat down beside him. He laid his head on her shoulder. Her body filled with warmth, the type that she always imagined would come from the fire if she ever stepped into it, radiating from the outside in and back again. She didn't know if she smiled but she hoped she did, hoped she glowed some iridescent color that lit the room and warmed James as much as she felt comfortable now. She tilted her head against his.

"Thank you," he said.

"You would have done the same," she said.

"Stop," he said. "Accept the credit. Thank you."

"You're welcome." For a brief moment she sat next to him in a bubble without the fear of the outside world breaking through: no snow, no Abe, no settlement, no deer, no dogs, nothing but them in a tiny shack they called home. "We can call today your birthday."

"It's not like we'll remember it next year," he said with a weak laugh. His voice was racked with gravel.

"Do you need some water?"

"I'm fine," he said. "I let Abe go."

She had forgotten about the body tied and stuffed in the corner. A deep breath released that she didn't even know she had taken, a breath stuck between relief and shame, part anger and part uncertainty. "Why? What are we going to do? Why would you do that? What did he say?" Too many questions needed to be answered. They spilled out of her all at once with the hope that James would have all the answers, simply because he was there, he had let Abe go, and he woke up in time to make a decision so she wouldn't have to. When hard choices came around it was easier to let someone else make the decisions and take all the blame. She wasn't proud of it. She was more than a stone throw's away from where she ever thought she would be in her lifetime. To even have to contemplate whether or not she would kill someone, more than the mere hyperbole of saying it, turned her stomach and tightened her chest like an undoable knot.

"I couldn't do it," James said. They didn't look at each other but stared at the endless smoke drifting upwards from the old fire. She almost moved to recreate the flames and give a little more heat to the cave, but James hadn't been awake for days and she wanted to revel in this moment a little longer, perhaps forever.

She wanted to ask the obvious question, "Do what?" but she knew what James couldn't do because she couldn't do it either.

"I know," she said.

"I didn't even have to," James said. "I could have left him there, tied up, and it would have taken care of itself."

"What?"

"He might have been hurt, I don't know, but the longer he laid there the less he could breathe. He still tried to talk to me. The harder he tried the harder it was for me to let him stay there, tied like an animal, suffocating. I was just going to loosen the rope but it came undone and I—I couldn't do it."

Some lives are harder than others, Charlotte thought, *but taking two lives that saw so much hardship and bringing them that much more is unfair.*

"Were you at Fornland when we played war?" James asked.

"I saw some of the young kids play once," Charlotte said. The air started to smell of roasted meat that must have come through the halls. Breakfast would be served soon.

"Abe and I started that game. At least what it became. I don't remember Abe ever wanting to be remembered; mostly I remember him wanting to be forgotten, invisible. But when we played that game we were invincible in so many ways. It was just pure fun and forgetting. We didn't have to think about anything except winning."

"Sounds like fun."

"I think Abe is worried about winning now."

"This isn't a game."

"I know."

"You shouldn't have let him go," Charlotte said. It was the first time she admitted it to herself, let alone James; it was far easier to criticize a decision after it was done, after she excused herself from making one at all. She looked into the corner and reached for James's hand. He didn't wear any gloves. His fingers were frail and skeletal. The corner where

Abe had lain was hauntingly empty. Franklin stared through his beady black eyes.

"I know," he said.

"Why did you let him go?"

"For the same reason you would have. We aren't him. We can't forget that."

"Tic-Tac doesn't want to be in the settlement anymore."

"He shouldn't have been there this long," James said.

"We need to figure out what to do next," she said.

The ship was less safe now than it had ever been. They would find someplace to hide, to continue living, because now more than ever they couldn't go back to the settlement. Now more than ever they had to figure out how they could survive anywhere else on the island.

"We have to take whoever wants to come with us," Charlotte said.

"I know."

"I have a plan," she said. "You know Abe best, though. What do you think he's going to do?"

"We need to leave soon."

"Not without paying them a visit first."

"Go on," James said.

Charlotte pulled herself away from James and finally looked into his sunken, dark eyes. "You're too thin." They both were, they both knew it, but he had spent the last however many days or weeks unconscious to Charlotte's touch and the warmth and the cold and the despair and the happiness, closed off to a world that she needed him to be a part of. "We need to fix that."

"I think you're right."

"Smells like breakfast is ready," Charlotte said. "There are some new faces you need to see."

"Let's see some new faces then."

"First you need to put on your clothes," she said.

They stepped out of the room and through the hallway. The outer beauty of the ocean scenery once filled the windows, decorating the dining room like paintings. Now the space echoed with remnants of the past fire. Ash was etched into the molding and walls. The structure had caved inward where the windows once stood. The windows had shattered and the ceiling arched from side to side, keeping the snow out and the space open but lowered. When they stepped into the hall, all the faces looked at James and merged into a solitary glance of quiet hope. Maybe it wasn't too late after all. They made their way to the front of the room where a pot of stew steamed. Phil handed the hot bowl to James.

"You're looking good," Phil said.

"You're full of shit," James said. "Thanks for the food." Charlotte took his bowl and held hers as well, guiding James to an open space for them to sit. He coughed under the weight of clothes he hadn't worn in far too long, with the blanket wrapped around him like a robe. He coughed once more, and again, until he stared at the floor, ready to fall into it.

"You're okay," Charlotte said. She stated it because she wanted to believe it more than anything.

"I'm fine," he said, "just too excited for the food." He took his bowl, sipped at the rim, and the sounds of the room started to come to life. He didn't look strong enough to hold the bowl. Charlotte watched in case he needed help, but that word never came out of his mouth. Was it pride or did he believe he could make it through life without anyone else? When James had slept for days, drained of the strength to even blink, Charlotte had asked for help, voicing hopeful words to the air, to the fire, to Franklin, the ice, in the hopes that something would open James's eyes. Did he think he was strong enough to hold all his problems inside? Charlotte believed strength was the courage to ask for help when needed; maybe he didn't *need* the help. But she'd be here just in case.

ACCEPTING
FATE

ABE

THIS WAS WHERE MADNESS BEGAN—WITH THE FRIGID LOSS of all Abe had once held close, and without the reasons everyone else had that Abe felt only pushed him away. It had started earlier, long ago when all he wanted was to disappear like the invisible children who could fade into walls and never look back. Soon enough everyone noticed Abe. He didn't know what to do with the attention.

He acted in a way he thought he should act but not in a way he wanted to act.

Both boys and girls would ask him about his day, "Did you see the new board at Crawleys?" "Did you take a shot on the boardwalk?" "How was

Mr. Abraham's halitosis?" The questions didn't matter and Abe most often nodded his head in some indefinable way with a small grimace, less of an assault on the question than a subtle admittance of indifference. "That's badass," some of the older kids would say. Some of the smaller kids would cross their arms and try to imitate the passive look on Abe's face. He and James often read near the window in one of the common rooms where books lined the walls. Not many other people ever visited, unless James read a story out loud or the scent of pizza brought a crowd by.

Now Abe sat in the greenhouse by the window and dreamt about the days alone in Fornland, sitting by the window reading an adventure story about a fantastical world built on a desert island. He watched the plants lazily drift toward the direction of the sun, whichever way it shined through the window. If he was still enough, he could see the leaves drift and sway in the direction of the light reaching for nutrients. He had been taken and was gone from dusk to dawn. Over a day had passed and he wanted anyone to notice he was missing; no one had, at least not anyone left in the settlement. Only those who were no longer around knew he had been gone at all.

"You wanted to see me?" Tic-Tac entered the greenhouse.

"Close the door," Abe said. "Don't want that steam to get out."

The humid air of the greenhouse revitalized some of the indigenous plants, along with some of the plants they carried from the ship, herbs they reutilized that ate up the misty air and heat. Abe had to know if it was Tic-Tac who was out in the woods the other night.

Exhaustion clouded over him. The common misconception about passing out was that the person was asleep. When Abe woke up he had felt more tired than anything, groggy with half-open eyes and a lustful need to drift back into some restful state that was now too late to reach. The sounds of breakfast rang from the dining hall, kids ready for the day and hungry from the night. The powdered eggs had run dry months earlier. Breakfast was usually some sort of soup or stew filled with vegetables and meat, a necessary heartiness that helped the settlement get moving in the morning.

"It was you," Abe said. "Wasn't it?"

"What was me?" Tic-Tac asked. He brushed his fingers against the leafy herbs that grew and dangled.

"The other night," Abe said. "The shadowy figures." Abe drew up his hands and wiggled his fingers to seem less intimidating. People had started to stare at Abe's black fingertip. He had started to hide it but soon felt it gave him an unexpected upper hand. He didn't care that Tic-Tac had been out in the woods at night to meet Sarah. He would have done the same thing if it were he and Elise. He needed to know if Tic-Tac made progress on finding who supplied the outliers, and now he needed to know if Tic-Tac had seen anything.

"Don't be stupid," Abe said. "You saved my life, I'm sure."

"I needed to see her," Tic-Tac said. "It was like, if I didn't see her I just didn't want to get up the next day."

"It's okay," Abe said. "I know that feeling. I'm stuck with that feeling more than ever, opening my eyes before the sun breaks and questioning whether I want to get out of bed at all. Worse on those days when I dream of Elise, her dark hair draped over the bed, her soft body there—I can feel it. Then I wake up and she isn't there. Those are the worst days."

"I have similar dreams . . . fears," Tic-Tac said.

"What's your real name?" Abe asked. "I never knew."

"It doesn't matter," Tic-Tac said.

"Don't say that. Of course it does."

Tic-Tac grabbed a basil leaf, pulled it from the stem and sniffed it. It was fresh and damp, Abe knew, as though it sweat in the heat like the rest of them.

"It doesn't though," Tic-Tac said. "That life before now—before Fornland even—I wasn't anyone. It was a life I never got a chance to know in some world I never understood, and probably never will." Tic-Tac took a bite out of the basil and tore away the leafy edge.

"When was the last time you saw this much green?" Abe asked. "I love it in here. It reminds me of . . . I don't even know what. The color just makes me happy, you know? I can come in here no matter how the day goes and just feel better about things. The fact the plants grew at all is something like a miracle."

"That's how legends are made," Tic-Tac said.

"I like that," Abe said. "It's true. That is how legends are made." Abe lifted the jagged edge of a small palm they had planted. Life perseveres when it can. When they planted the tree they didn't know if it would bear any fruit at all; now he could pull of a bunch of bananas and peel open the creamy, semi-sweet fruit. Sometimes to bear fruit he just needed to plant a seed and hope for the best, then peel it back slowly until it gave him what he wanted. "I guess you could say this greenhouse is the stuff of legends. Kind of like your need to see Sarah. You went through feral dog-infested jungle, man. Not the smartest choice."

"You followed me," Tic-Tac said. His eyes looked past Abe, through the window, into the light that struck over the trees and made his pupils thin, fragile, and searching.

"Not the smartest decision I ever made," Abe said. "But I thought it might have been whoever's been helping the outliers. Thought you had your coat stuffed with food or spoons or something."

"Can't say that I did."

"Any progress on that?"

"Stuffing my coat with spoons?"

"Finding out who it might be," Abe said. "It's been a few days. I'm not sure if anything more's gone missing. I haven't had the chance to take a look, but every day someone helps them we lose some of our needed resources. We can't just let people take what's ours."

"To be fair they helped bring that stuff out of the ship too. All of this is from them too, especially this greenhouse. Wouldn't have done it without Charlotte."

Tic-Tac gave Abe a direct and uncompromising look. Abe knew Tic-Tac had his ways of forcing his opinion down people's throats. Or through their eyes.

"Did you find them or not?"

"It's going to take more time to find him," Tic-Tac said.

"Who said it was a *him*?" Abe asked.

"I meant it as all-encompassing—him, her, them."

"It should have been a them. It's one person? One guy? You know who it is, don't you?" Abe blocked the sunlight with his head. He wanted to look straight into Tic-Tac's eyes and see who would come out the victor of a staring contest when truth was the prize.

"No," Tic-Tac said. "I don't." He stood

straighter. His pupils opened up to the look of the greenhouse. He didn't blink, didn't budge. Tic-Tac's eyes were brown boulders that rolled into Abe attempting to move him. Abe wouldn't move, not now. By not moving Abe could tell Tic-Tac lied; Tic-Tac gave himself away by trying to push Abe down with his look, whether he knew it or not.

"You," Abe said.

"I don't know who it was."

"It was you." Tic-Tac was the one person left Abe thought he could trust, the one person left from a time before they all drifted in indifferent directions, and the oscillation of Tic-Tac between hopeful and hopeless gave Abe confidence that Tic-Tac could be trusted. Trust didn't exist anymore, from Tic-Tac to James, down to Elise, who never said how she had felt or thought, to the point of oblivion dripping down her fucking wrists. "It was you!"

Abe leapt toward Tic-Tac, kicking the table behind him and driving Tic-Tac to the floor. Tic-Tac's height didn't matter; his size didn't matter;

his friendship didn't matter. All that mattered were Abe's hands wrapped around Tic-Tac's neck. Tic-Tac hit Abe's arms, balled his fingers into fists and hit Abe's elbows and kicked his legs. Tic-Tac flailed his feet. His eyes looked like glass balls ready to break open and ooze shit onto his face. Abe had to squeeze harder. Skin and bone felt soft between his fingers, beneath his seething anger. Every time Tic-Tac swallowed, Abe felt his grip contract a little tighter, a boa constrictor in a sheltered jungle strangling its prey one breath at a time.

"You're a liar!" Abe said. "A rotten liar!" The plants were silent, leaning once again toward the sunlight. Abe didn't matter to them; Tic-Tac didn't matter to them. All they needed was light. The light didn't touch Abe as he sat on top of Tic-Tac's chest and watched the life creep out of Tic-Tac's body. "Now they're all going to die. Tonight. That's how it's going to end, with James looking like you—afraid. We're all afraid to die aren't we? That's why we stick around like nasty, frozen shit, defiant until it's wiped away. But I'll still be here."

The door swung open and Autry walked in. She turned around the table and found Abe hovered over Tic-Tac and she screamed. Her cry was shrill and rang in Abe's ears in an endless reverberation. It felt like a blink before Tic-Tac pushed Abe away. He struggled for breath, grabbed Autry's arm, and bolted from the greenhouse. He didn't close the door.

Abe stood up and saw Tic-Tac make his way to the trees with Autry trying to keep up behind him. The settlement ate in the dining hall ready to start the day; some had already streamed out of the doors for work.

"What's happening?" asked Kelsey, one person in a handful of people lingering in the square.

"Tic-Tac attacked me," Abe said. "He's been helping the others."

Kelsey gasped. She hadn't noticed when Abe had crept out of the settlement or back into it, he realized; *no one had noticed.* Now Abe didn't care if people noticed or not, he needed to get people on his side.

"We're going after them," he said. "Tonight. Get ready."

"He took Autry with him," Kelsey said. "Shouldn't we be cautious?"

"It's too late for that. He took her, he's been helping them, and now they all have to be punished. It's law." He spat out the last words in a sneer, filled with a pleasurable hatred that tasted sweet on his tongue.

Abe walked back to his room through the loud murmur of the settlement. This was his island. People needed to know that, and the outliers would learn that the hard way. Soon the settlement would be at war, taking back what belonged to them— what belonged to Abe: everyone. Everyone belonged to Abe.

THICKER
THAN WATER
TIC-TAC

THE JUNGLE FELT THICKER THAN USUAL, WHERE TREES BECAME more than frozen wood and frozen leaves; they stretched over the sky and became a new world filled with an abundance of shade—not the shade that helped people avoid the sun and keep them tanned instead of burnt in a summer Tic-Tac could barely remember, but a tarp that covered the sky and turned this new world into darkness. Tic-Tac climbed through the shadows with Autry behind him, trying to push aside the black sky and heavy brush that never seemed this thick when he had hunted or gone to meet Charlotte, to find Sarah, or to venture through some new place to find himself on an island that had lost so many.

"I'm cold," Autry said.

"I know," Tic-Tac said with all the compassion he could find. The sweat was a sheet on his skin and when hit by the breeze, it started to crackle with frost. He moved slower with Autry, needing to drag her tiny body with every fourth step to keep her moving. She didn't want to go with him but they didn't have a choice. If she stayed in the settlement she would have been in danger. He needed to take her with him to the ship; he needed to warn the others. No one would be safe there either. The mood of the island had changed, shifting somewhere between the overwhelming color of nothing and a tangible blood red Tic-Tac swore he saw in the sky. He had wanted to leave the settlement anyway, but he never imagined this. If it weren't for Autry . . .

"We're going to be okay," he said with a calm,

cold breath. "We're going to see Charlotte. She could use your help."

"Is Teagan coming?" Autry asked.

"Later," he lied. "He'll come later." Would Teagan come later? Would he be able to, or would Abe have Teagan killed, publically maimed, jailed, or whatever sadistic punishment Abe could think of? Teagan's sister was in the wrong place at the wrong time and inadvertently helped Tic-Tac. No matter what Tic-Tac did, someone would get hurt, himself or Autry, Teagan or Charlotte. Safety had frozen over and sunk beneath the island.

"We'll be at the ship soon," he lied again. The jungle didn't look the same. The small markings that the outliers used to make their way through the dense trees were hidden or gone. The maze made every twist and turn look the same, keeping him from the far side of the island and from a moment of rest. Once they had hit the tree line they ran and ran without a glance back to the settlement in case someone heard or saw Abe crying out for help. The ship was Tic-Tac and Autry's only hope for survival and he would be damned if he wouldn't make it another day after all the days he had struggled to survive up to this point already.

"You have to keep up," he said.

"I'm tired," she said.

"We're almost there, I promise."

"Was that a dog?"

"It was the wind." His voice grumbled with aggravation, not from her but from the circumstance, annoyed that he had to drag her around with him, angry he couldn't find the tree marks that led to the ship, disappointed that he couldn't have done more to protect Autry, the ship, himself, and it all came through in his answers to Autry. "You don't have to worry about the wind." How many times could he lie to this girl? In a matter of minutes he'd told three. Did he think he was protecting her, or was he protecting himself?

Through the darkness he could make out a faint opening, not where light shone through but where the emptiness of shadows opened. He ran and pulled Autry behind him.

"It's there," he said.

"The wind sounds loud," she screamed over their desperate run. "I'm tired."

"It's just there," he said. "We can rest in a minute." He panted and pulled and ran and trudged, and pushed branches out of the way. The trees opened. The ship sat along the ice like a three-dimensional image of a silhouette, tangible but barely visible unless he looked out of the corner of his eye.

"Can we stop running now?"

"Yes," he said. "We can stop running now."

They walked through the open icy stretch, through the gaping hole in the ship's remainder and into the cavernous halls.

He went to Sarah's room and found it empty. He went to Charlotte's room and found the same. He listened for an echoed voice, a simple noise, a rumble from the dining hall—nothing.

"Where is everyone?" Autry asked.

"Sarah?" Tic-Tac called. "Charlotte?" Silence responded. They stepped through the burnt-out halls and knocked on the walls and the doors hoping to hear a voice call out, footsteps running, any sound that proved someone was present. Abe couldn't have made it here before them but it didn't account for where everyone else was. The ship was empty, no denying it.

"We can rest now?" Autry asked.

"No," Tic-Tac said. "I'm sorry but we can't."

"But you said."

Tic-Tac knelt down. His knee cracked and felt rigid. He fought the urge to grunt as he came face to face with Autry.

"We can't rest, yet. I need you to run one more time."

"But I don't want to. Where's Charlotte?" Autry's eyes looked into Tic-Tac's. She didn't search the room with the hope someone might step out of the corners or the doors. She didn't show any fear, but it was a moment to be afraid.

"I don't want to either," Tic-Tac said.

"Then why do we have to?"

Tic-Tac raised his gloved hand to Autry's cheek and brushed away flecks of frost that clung to her chubby skin.

"Sometimes we have to do things we don't understand or don't want to do. Sometimes it protects us from danger and fear."

"But you said I didn't have to be afraid of the wind," she said.

"I know," he said. "But I was wrong." He held her face with both hands; she might better understand him if he somehow held her close. Her eyes were blue, the color of the sky on a warm day near the water, days that didn't exist anymore. It was comforting to look into her eyes even if it was the only comfort he would find for the moment, the day, the rest of his life, however long that would be.

157

"The wind can be scary. It howls and pushes but it's what it carries that we fear."

"What's that?" Autry's voice whispered beneath the aches of Tic-Tac's fear. Her flush cheeks reminded him of his sister, the last time he saw her, moments before the house erupted. She had looked tired but attentive, her tone and eyes sincere. She could have fallen asleep at that moment, sitting up, with the book in her hands and the hot southern-California air falling over their house. Autry looked ready to close her eyes and rest her head on any surface, the smoky wall or frigid floor, and pass the night in unencumbered sleep. If Tic-Tac could have, he would have left Autry there to rest. The world closed in on them and they needed to outrun it.

"The wind carries people away and can bring danger closer," Tic-Tac said.

"What is it doing now?"

"Both," he said. "And we need to outrun the wind right now. You understand?" His voice took on a softness he didn't know he had. For a second he believed they would be safe, too. Through the combination of his tone and her eyes, he almost believed they could run to a day that existed before now and sit on a sandy beach with a warm sky and a brilliant sun and breaking waves that would wash over them. They couldn't stay on the ship, not when Abe would soon flood through the doors. Everyone else was gone. Tic-Tac and Autry were alone. They had to survive somehow. They had to run somewhere. It wouldn't save them tomorrow but it would save them right now.

"You ready?" he asked. Autry nodded and they ran into the trees.

IN PLAIN SIGHT

ABE

Abe didn't care about the light, whether they would be seen or noticed; he wanted to be seen, to be noticed. He made the entire settlement come with him, young and younger, hurt and broken, those who wanted rest or were hungry—even Rachel, who was still recovering from her wounds from being strung up in the square, had to come. The settlement needed to experience—needed to witness—what happened to outliers, liars, abandoners, and thieves. The torches brought the jungle into daylight as they made their way through the trees. Their steps and breaths and whispers ran around the canopy beneath a roaring crackle of the fire they brought with them. Abe would burn the ship to the ground if the outliers wouldn't come with him, if anyone refused at all. It was all or nothing.

Kelsey marched beside Abe with a slanted smirk that glared against her fiery skin. She moved closer to him with every step and Abe tried to ignore her and how close she came to him. He focused on the trees, the bark, and the movement of the night that looked like a day filled with sun; he hadn't seen the sun in far too long. How could darkness glow so bright? All it took was a little bit of fire to bring a rage of color to the absence of pigment. Young kids cried beneath the flickering warmth, tired or hungry. Abe didn't care. Soon they would be at the ship reclaiming those and that which belonged to the settlement—to Abe—and he would collect what he was owed.

The rumbling quiet of the people flittered through the trees, overcome by the torches, the night, and the fact that Abe hadn't shared his plan with anyone, only that they all needed to venture out to protect themselves. Tic-Tac had attacked Abe, through his deceit. It was an attack on the entire settlement, stolen food and goods that belonged to everyone given away for a stupid girl who couldn't take the troubles they all had to deal with. Tic-Tac was a lovesick puppy, attached to a weakling. He put his heart on the path and hoped it wouldn't get stepped on or frozen over. Abe wanted to laugh at him, shame him for his stupidity. Abe couldn't help but think of Elise and how she didn't last, couldn't last. But she had been stronger, stronger than Sarah, Abe knew. How had Sarah lasted this long, this person who lacked will, strength, power, fortitude? What did Sarah have that Elise didn't, that made Tic-Tac cling to her instead of to the settlement that needed him? Tic-Tac turned his back on them stupidly, selfishly. He had to pay for his crimes, Sarah had to pay for making him do it, Charlotte for enduring and perpetuating the theft, and James for all the wrong he had done. The ship would burn and they would pay.

The crowd brandished weapons, some with bows wrapped around their backs, others wielding spears carved from tree bark and shaped into splintered, sharp points. There was an occasional metal tip at the edge of an arrow or spear from the metal they had taken and shaped from the ship's interior, whatever they could scrape away and mold to their needs. Abe wanted weapons for the settlement's safety in case they needed to hunt or had to fend off dogs. In the back of his mind he imagined an uprising from young or inexperienced kids who didn't know better, but he could never have imagined this. He was glad he had the weapons..

"Grab half the knives from the kitchen," Abe had said.

"But that's—" Shia said.

"That's what?" Abe asked.

"Against the rules."

"Not anymore," Abe said. "Not for this."

"What is this?" Shia asked.

"War."

"We need to eat with those . . . though." Shia stood straight, chest barely puffed out in an act of defiance in the dwindling gray of the daylight.

"Now is not the time to grow a backbone," Abe said. Shia cowered a little, retreating back into himself, his shoulders hunched, eyes unfocused. "Get Teagan. Tell him Tic-Tac kidnapped his sister and used her like a shield to escape, like a coward. Teagan will probably volunteer his knives. We don't eat with those do we?"

"No," Shia mumbled.

"No what?"

"We don't. I'll get Teagan," Shia had said.

The snow was thick around Abe's feet, wrapped around his ankles when he stepped forward. "Keep moving," he called out. "Anyone who stays behind will be considered part of the enemy."

Older girls held close to smaller children, helping them step in the bundled snow. The smaller kids were huddled in wraps, their clothes still not big enough to cover all of them and clothes in general too scarce to use for repairs. Tired boys trudged along the trees. Some of the larger boys who hadn't had to walk in snow this deep pressed their hands to the bark for support, lingered in the back, and slogged with exaggerated grunts. The smaller kids trailed in the middle, curious and scared from the looks that flashed on their faces. The braver and more foolish kids led the pack, behind Abe, with weapons in their hands—girls, guys, anyone who could hold a bow or a stick, or knew how to force their way into a room and push out those who needed pressing.

They came to the clearing, the space between the jungle and the boat. Abe halted everyone at the border.

"Get in and push them out," he said. "If they refuse—make them." The flames rushed under the canopy and brought a fractured burn to the night. They pressed closer to the ship. In this light Abe couldn't see his breath. As they came closer to the ship, his walk turned into a jog and the jog turned into a run. The settlement ran behind him, some even pushed passed him, including Kelsey who seemed the most eager to get into the ship and bring the outliers home. It was the first time Abe had seen the ship since he set it ablaze, after they had arrived.

The proud vessel he had found in San Diego was a ghost of itself, a shroud of muddled gray, similar to the dead sky, a lingering reminder of an inaccessible past. The gaping hole in the bow looked like a mouth, sharp and screaming. It called to Abe with resentment, a burial ground for their hopes, and also for Captain, the first life Abe had taken, for the good of the group, to ensure their survival. They didn't need a *man*. They needed one another. Abe had pulled the trigger and watched the life quickly drain from Captain. He doused the ship in gasoline without remorse. He would do the same to James in the halls where this fucked-up journey began.

They reached the open hole at the ship's hull. The flaming torches fanned through the hallways, knocking into doors, the dining room. The foul stench of thieves filled each open space. Abe came to the room he had called a prison for one day of his life. The rope that had seared into his skin was absent from the corner, now filled only with empty cold. The fire had long been put out. The ship was empty of anyone.

"Where did they go?" he asked. Even if Tic-Tac had gotten here immediately after he left, it wouldn't have been enough time for all the outliers to leave with no trace of smoke. "Did you find someone?" He turned to Shia who stood with a long carved spear in his hand that was taller than him. Shia shook his head. "You," he pointed to Kelsey, "anyone?"

"No one's here," she said.

"How can they all be gone?"

No one moved. The fire didn't even crackle. In the cavernous ship stood one of the loudest silences Abe had ever heard. He looked back at the sullen and quiet faces of the settlement that he dragged with him to the vacant, cold ship they all wanted to forget. They didn't all need to be here, but stories wouldn't be enough anymore. Stories were lies James had told to get them all to the island, fill their heads with happy endings that didn't exist in real life. They needed to see what real life made and how real life made them; the cold and the settlement weren't enough. Stories were lies but legends lived forever.

"I'm sorry I brought you all here tonight," Abe said. "We should go back. We will find them later."

"Sorry?" Kelsey said. "But—"

"There is no reason to stay here and wait for them to come back in this cold. We will form a search party tomorrow. The rest of you will stay behind and stay safe in the settlement." He said it to Kelsey, a person who had never questioned him before and he wouldn't let her start now. The melting-lipped smile faded away. The roar of the collected torches came back to life. Abe stepped out of the ship and the settlement followed with soft steps on the supple snow.

WHEN THE SETTLEMENT'S AWAY...

JAMES

THE OUTLIERS FOLLOWED JAMES THROUGH THE TREES ALONG the back pathway to the settlement. At the other end of the expansive freeze they saw a glowing light that lifted and fell, the way the Northern Lights used to shift when they filled the sky and cut out the stars. No one asked what the light might be but James knew some of them wanted to get close to the fire and stick their hands in it, let the heat sink into their skin after stuck so long in the endless cold. Instead he and Charlotte pushed forward through the woods, distancing themselves from the slithering orb of color, and arriving on the fringe of the homes they had all helped to build. Everyone ducked down so as not to be caught lurking in the trees. The homes and build-ings were as silent and dark as the forest before the smattering of light broke through. A few of the smaller kids whimpered with misunderstanding, not knowing why they had stopped, cold and fragile as they had ever been, as all of them were, but the older kids at least knew what they ran from and what they ran for.

Charlotte tried to shush the smattering of whim-pers and whispers; the sounds didn't grow louder but they didn't stop, either.

"We need as many hands as we can get," Charlotte said in a whisper, which passed back to the farthest reaches of the line like a glass of hot water. People raised their hands to volunteer.

They had brought everyone from the ship, includ-ing Franklin, who was shoved deep inside the sack Charlotte held. Not everyone could help; not every-one had the hands or the stealth to burst through the settlement unseen and gain access to the granary, the greenhouse, slip what they needed into their bags, and sprawl out at the edges of the village to not be

discovered. James said they needed to bring everyone anyway, for they all knew they needed to leave
the ship behind fast. Charlotte had the idea to raid
the settlement. Beyond the raid and the move, they
weren't sure what would become of them. *We survived in the open with Robert and we can do it again,*
James thought. *At least until we find something better.*

Charlotte picked eight hands out of the crowd, a
combination of speed and strength, to grab as much as
they could as fast as they could. James stood up to go.

"You stay," Charlotte said.

"I want to help," he said.

"You've done so much already. You're not recov-
ered yet and we need someone here to help keep
everyone together and ready to go."

"I can go with you. I'm good for it." *The hardest part about a sickness is admitting to yourself that
you lost a bit of who you were before,* James thought.
He couldn't concede that he lost a step and some
strength. If he admitted that he would be admitting
he wasn't the same person; somehow it changed him

in ways he couldn't imagine if he allowed himself to agree.

Charlotte grabbed his hand. His fingers were frail and thin. A cough swirled around in his lungs before he had to spit it out. *Sometimes the world makes you believe something before you're ready to,* James thought. He knew Charlotte was right, he needed to stay.

"Be safe," James said.

"As if I need you to tell me that," Charlotte said with a sly smile. Her hair dangled around her chest. The white strands wrapped up and around her body before twisting in the brown and disappearing beneath her beanie. "We'll be back soon. Keep everyone quiet and awake." She took the eight volunteers she had chosen. "We all know the points. Run, get in, take whatever you can carry." They all nodded. Charlotte stood from her crouch and headed straight for the greenhouse with a sack flailing by her side.

When the wind blew and the dogs howled, jolts and gasps rose from the kids behind James. He tried to follow the fast-moving silhouettes that flew through the settlement. When they left, they had all seemed guarded but now many of them seemed less cautious, no longer hiding behind walls or peering around corners. They walked openly through the square, at least from what James could see of them, taking slow, wide strides like conquerors in their new kingdom. Phil and Cheryl carried their large bags next to the committee building. Cheryl spit on the door. James couldn't tell if their bags were filled. Phil unbuttoned his pants and dipped as he pulled out his penis before he started to piss all over the door. Steam rose from where the hot stream hit the cold snow.

"Where is everyone?" James asked himself. As he said the words he heard Daron behind him.

"No one's there." She didn't say the words to him; they drifted behind him and covered the group, young and younger. She stood up and ran out to the square, followed by more. "No one's here!" she yelled, her arms spread out, head titled up in a premature victory celebration.

"Wait," James said in a whisper. He tried to wave

them all back and keep new people from joining the crowd. They wanted to dance in the open square like the victors they weren't but they didn't hear him, didn't see him, or just ignored him.

"Charlotte's going to be pissed," Sarah said. She kneeled next to James.

"Where is everyone?" James asked.

"If they aren't here I don't know what to tell you."

"It looks like no one is here, including—"

"I know," Sarah said. "I don't know where he could be."

"We need to round them up," James said. "Wherever everyone is, I doubt they'll be gone— unless . . . "

They stood up and entered the crowd of kids that hung around the open square, tapping on windows and pushing open doors. Some kids entered the dining hall and laid down on the tables, Daron included.

"We need to go," James said. "We can't stay here."

"It's so warm," Daron said. "I forgot how warm it could be." She didn't take off her coat. None of them took off their clothes and basked in the heat that sprung from the floors. It felt like an old, comfortable blanket. James didn't want to leave it either. Why couldn't they just step into the settlement and take over? They wouldn't have to reshape a new community for themselves built out of igloos and ice fishing or some damn crazed institution like that. They could all wash over the settlement like a river and take it, pushing out what was. *You can't move a river.*

"What the hell are you doing?" Charlotte asked. Her bag looked fat and heavy. She stood behind James in the cold air outside of the dining hall. James wanted to let the door fall away like a sheet. Instead Charlotte took over the door, blocking the trees in the distance, a reminder of what they were there for and the fact they needed to leave.

"You were supposed to keep everyone in the trees."

"I know," he said. "It just happ—we need to get them out of here."

"Is this because I wouldn't let you come with?" Charlotte asked.

"No," James said. "It just happened. I tried to keep—"

"It doesn't matter. Sarah said she saw that fire far in the jungle, but it's coming closer. We need to go. Fast and quiet, okay?"

James nodded and rounded up Daron and the others lingering in the dining hall. He collected Phil and Cheryl along the way as Sarah and Charlotte grabbed the others.

"Mind your zipper," Daron told Phil.

"Don't mind at all," Phil said.

Some of those not chosen for reconnaissance had taken silverware that now poked out of their pockets, pots they wore on their heads; a few pretended to fight with spears and bows they took from the armory.

"Where'd you get those?" James asked Lewis. Lewis had been one of the youngest kids in

Fornland before they ventured away from San Diego. His parents gave up on him after they gave up on each other, neither one wanting to raise a kid who reminded them too much of the other. James had read that in Lewis's file. It was amazing how brutally honest people were when they thought no one would see.

"We found them," Lewis said. "Not much left."

"Show me," James said.

"Shouldn't we leave them something?" Sarah said. "They need to live too."

"We're just taking what we can," Charlotte said. "We're not trying to leave them dry."

Lewis pointed and James found the armory almost depleted of the weapons he knew had been there.

"Shit," he said. "We really need to go." The fire burned between the trees like a San Diegan inferno bringing a dreaded firestorm closer to them. James ran to tell Charlotte about the armory. "I know where everyone went. That fire is them and they're coming right for us."

"Get moving!" Charlotte said, no longer trying to keep her voice to a whisper. Everyone needed to get together and get out. "If you're not collected in the next ten seconds, you're left behind. We'll have to let Abe deal with you." A crashing quiet fell over them all, the harsh realization of the moments to come and what they had done by not staying in safety's reach.

"Where can we go?" Daron asked. "What can we do?"

"We shouldn't have all come out," Sarah said.

"That's not going to help," James said.

"He's right," Charlotte said. "We need to get going now, back to the trees where we came from. Once the fire is gone we can make our way deeper into the jungle."

"They'll find us," Phil said.

"Not if you follow us," Charlotte said.

"And stop pissing everywhere," Cheryl said. "They'll just follow the stench."

Charlotte grabbed James's hand and they made their way to the trees together. The rest of the outliers followed. James swore he could hear the collected heartbeat of everyone pulsing like a drum circle, adding a well-needed rhythm to the night as they tried to demand their freedom from the lives they never wanted, to create more for themselves. The imagined heartbeats gave way to a hopeful scream—the imagined furious cry of Abe when he found out what James had done. They reached the trees and hid in the dark depths of the snowy bark. James smiled. They could survive tonight; they could die tonight, but no matter what, at least they could hold their heads up and know they had lived, even for a breath, without fear, even as they hid within the jungle.

FORTRESS
OF FROZEN WOOD

JAMES

THE TREES SAT OVER THEM LIKE WALLS THAT FORMED, MOVED, and shaped their maze, trapping them like rats on an island where animals were scarce but never far from their minds. The flames came closer on the outskirts of their labyrinth with the crackle and flicker of light louder than any thunder James had ever heard, louder than the last gasp of air he heard Geoff gargle before James slid the blade into Geoff's broken chest and watched the light fade from his eyes. How dark that light had been in the first place until it fizzled like spit on smoldering wood. Here the flames wound around the walls, broke apart from the long, single line of orange and yellow James thought it was, into individual torches of smoky wood with people attached, Abe in front, Kelsey with her head down by his side, Shia lingering behind and the entire settlement sloping backwards in the light.

The torches guided the people through the trees and into the open air near the greenhouse, where the path began. Abe stopped with a short burst. His arms stretched out as he sniffed the air, like a dog smelling rancid fear mixed with some perverse sense of victory. Phil had left the scent on the committee door with the rest of the liquid he had sprayed, an animal marking its territory.

"Can he sm—" Cheryl said and was shushed by the group that made the huddled mass sound like sea spray instead of hidden refugees in search of safety, unsure how to flee. The entire fire ceased its movement through the jungle. James wanted to stand up and push everyone deeper into the trees, but they would be spotted.

"They were here," Abe said. James couldn't see

the look on Abe's face but he heard it. He'd known Abe long enough to see Abe's face by the tone of his voice. The controlled tone made Abe's rage scarier, the calm before the storm. "Check the granary."

Four flames separated from the pack and ran through the village. James's footprints, Charlotte's and Sarah's and everyone else's footprints would betray them as much as the stocks they had emptied. James hadn't thought about the prints they left behind, not thinking that a smart kid could tell the explosive number of feet that had tread through the village.

"The storage has been tampered with," a boy called out to Abe, from building to tree.

"Judging by the steps," the boy said, "and the intense smell of piss, we just missed them."

"If we just missed them then we could still catch them," Abe said. "I promised we would come back. Get the young ones and the injured ones inside. Rachel." Everyone paused. James heard the settlement's hesitation in the midst of Abe's command. "Stay here and rest. You've done enough." Sincerity ran through his voice and for a brief moment James forgot he crouched in the woods hiding. "Everyone else, you know what's coming."

"Shit," Charlotte whispered to James. Her words were hot in his ear. "How are we going to get out of here?"

"Hopefully he'll go back into the trees. We can leave when the fire fades, make our way perpendicular to the flames."

"But—"

"We don't have a place to go, Charlotte. It's not like we'll be missing out on our trail back somewhere."

The quiet sounds of their voices felt more fragile than snowflakes caught on a hot surface, ready to fizzle and melt. Some young kids shivered/ James heard their teeth chatter against the flicker of distant light and the crashing footsteps of those desperate to make it back into the warmth where

James knew most of the outliers wished they could go.

ABE

Abe knew the outliers had been in the settlement before anyone told him. He could smell them, that putrid stench of endless desperation, not to mention their acidic body odor wrapped around a drape of shit Abe hadn't escaped from since James let him loose on the ship. No, they were somewhere near, close enough for Abe to find if they set out now. The young and infirm would slow them down. He could let them go home and it would make him look merciful and understanding. The rest of them would catch up to the outliers for the last time. They had tricked him earlier but not this time. Abe could taste how close they were in their icy stink. A howl rose up from the woods behind them. It didn't sound like a dog though; it shouted a call to the wild, to them all, an animal so different from them, a signal from an outlier maybe.

Abe told the weaker kids to go and those with weapons to follow him as he turned around and led with his torch outstretched, once more into the darkness. The trees were less haunted in the torchlight. Abe realized when he was stuck in James's room that he didn't want to become the darkness; darkness was overcome by light, which cast over the island every day. Even when the useless sun didn't make an appearance, light shined through and over the island.

Darkness was useless. Abe stepped over the branches, refused defeat by light. Light was powerless because it always faded. Abe wanted to transcend both light and dark into something more eternal, something that shaped and formed in the bodies of everyone everywhere, always present in people's thoughts and fears, happiness and pleasures. The torches guided him away from the settlement. He searched the air and the ground for signs, prints or smells that could get him closer to his last obstacle, the one thing that kept the settlement from greatness, the last living colony in the world, as far as they knew. They had the only human settlement left in their world and that was all that mattered now; no one had ever cared about them before, so why should they bother with the world outside? They had been shaped and gathered by Fornland and now they shaped and gathered the world. James couldn't stop that. They earned this—Abe earned this, the right to lead a world that was theirs and theirs alone. The snow didn't make a sound as he stepped. He floated, followed the single flame ahead of him toward the howl that rang through the jungle and called to him in its contrived symbolism, saying the settlers had returned and for James and the outliers to run— except there was nowhere to run, not anymore.

JAMES

The calls of the wild led the outliers from their hiding place as the flames drifted farther away. None of them spoke and the younger kids were too afraid to whimper. It reminded James of thunderstorms, when some kids would cry and others would look stoically out the window at the flashes of light; James was one of the latter. People had thought him brave or indifferent. In truth James had been too scared to move, which included screaming. Instead he sat on his bed and watched the bolts out the windows. When the light flickered, he would blink and it would scatter; it was the only time in the storm he felt he could do anything, and it came down to a blink. In the forest he needed to do more than blink and help bring these kids to safety, through the snow and along the wooden walls the trees made.

The moment felt too similar to San Diego, when he had run from the scavengers who tore through the city, who eventually caught up to him and tore through Marcus, and there had been nothing James could do.

They made their way through the trees as silent as ghosts, hoping the hazy light from the sunrise would continue to break the darkness. James and Charlotte stuck close together. Sarah was somewhere behind them herding the pack through the trees, bordered by the settlement. James prepared for inevitable screams and curses, hunters chasing them with bows and flying spears. The outliers moved in a straight line in the darkness. Small scrapes against the trees and broken, crystalized snow opened the night and closed in on them. How had life brought James to this place again, running away from hunters who wanted to take what he had, which was less now than it had been in San Diego? The longer he stayed on the island, the less he owned and the less he became. He had the clothes on his back and Charlotte by his side, which counted for more than the clothes considering he spent so many recent days held up inside a blanket with Charlotte wrapped around him. His happiest moments on the island all came from the simple touches, the moments that literally brought him back from the brink of death.

The light hovered on the horizon, scattered like a shattered sunrise unable to piece itself back together and finish the job. Something was wrong with the light. It didn't move one way or the other. It didn't fade or flicker, fall or rise. The color of the jungle stayed in a limbo between night and day, brought about by torches James realized had been stuck in the ground.

"Hold on," James said. "Something's wrong."

"What is it?" Charlotte asked. She tried to keep moving, continue into the secrets of the jungle.

James brought her to a stop with the rest of the outliers behind him.

"The torches haven't moved."

"Good," she said. "They aren't coming closer. We should keep going."

"I don't think that's it," he said.

Charlotte looked at the lingering torches along the horizon. "Oh no," she said.

She's right, James thought. *Oh no.*

CHOOSING
YOUR BATTLES
SARAH

SARAH NOTICED THEM FIRST, NOT THE TORCHES IN THE DIS-
tance but the stilted shapes that clung to the
trees in fear. At first she thought they must have
been awkwardly formed deer, the type that often
stood against the trees to eat from the low hanging branches or dug through the frozen soil to eat
the roots, but the closer she looked she saw that
the shapes of people, one tall, one short, a broader
person that must have been male and a small child,
boy or girl, she couldn't tell. The boy's hands
wrapped around the child with a protected grace
both strong and anxious, as they pressed into the
tree looking to hide from the oncoming sounds, the

mass of shapeless forms that came toward them, the outliers.

"Look," Sarah said to Daron. "There's someone in those trees." The group had stopped but no one was sure why. Perhaps it had something to do with the shapes in the trees. Sarah made her way to the front to tell Charlotte and James what she saw. She pushed through gentle whimpers and cold bodies that rubbed against one another for warmth in the icicles of their own breaths. Every step she took was a fight upstream, against the solid mass of indecision and fear, following those that stood with the natural response to run, but had enough sense left to remember they didn't know where to go.

"In the trees over there," Sarah whispered to Charlotte.

"I know," Charlotte said.

"You saw them?"

"They're hard to miss," James said.

"I almost missed them," Sarah said.

"We can't get around them," Charlotte said but to whom Sarah wasn't sure.

"We can't go back the way we came," James said.

"There are only two of them," Sarah said. "What's the problem?"

"What are you talking about?" Charlotte said. "Look." She pointed straight ahead, past the two shadows huddled against the tree and into the armed line of settlers pointing arrows and spears in their direction.

"Then who are they?" Sarah pointed to the people in question.

"I'm not sure, but they picked a terrible place to hide," James said.

"Is that . . . " Charlotte said. The words were never finished in the course of the outliers' stillness. Sarah felt the uncertainty of the world around her and the wonder that hadn't stopped jabbing at her mind. She tried to subdue them with thoughts about anything else, and the secret hope that somewhere she would find an answer to where Tic-Tac was.

ABE

"Time to pick a side," Abe said. "Come this way and all's well, Tic-Tac. You and Autry will be safe."

The line of outliers huddled beyond the tree where Tic-Tac stood frozen like a frightened deer. Was he the one who had called out to James? They found one another, but Abe found them first. He had told Kelsey to take a few people and line up the torches in the distance to make it look like they marched away. The stench never left the woods and Abe knew they were close. The call had subsided the closer the outliers came to Tic-Tac; it couldn't have been a coincidence.

"Choose," Abe said. "It shouldn't be that hard."

"It's not," Tic-Tac said. "It never was." Tic-Tac came out with his hands up with Autry hidden behind him. He took a few steps from the tree. For every step he took Autry took two, hidden by his waist. Her small legs shuffled behind his.

"We're taking them either way," Kelsey said. "You made the right choice." Abe didn't cut her off. The moment needed cohesion. If he didn't stand behind her even after she'd stepped over the line by talking to Tic-Tac like that--something that she hadn't earned--it would look bad on both their parts. Bad, because they would look broken and incapable of unity and rank. Tic-Tac had put in his time with the committee and deserved a trial, where they could find the facts and put this mess behind them. Autry hadn't helped him; she was innocent— wrong place, wrong time. He could take pity on her. Abe touched Kelsey's wrist and she stopped, took a step back and closer to Abe.

"They know we're here," Abe said. "Time to give up."

"No," Tic-Tac said. He turned and said something to Autry. She ran away into the far line of outliers and wrapped her arms around someone Abe assumed was Charlotte. The person pressed Autry close to her like a sister or a mother might. The taller woman kneeled and pressed her hands to the girl's face. Abe imagined the unnecessary comforts Charlotte spoke to Autry, that she was safe now, no reason to worry, she would soon crawl into bed and rest after the long day she had had rushing through the jungle. Autry was never in any danger; why couldn't anyone see that? What kind of monster did they think Abe was? He ruled and fought fair, lived by the rules. Tic-Tac turned around. A rush of air flew past Abe. He knew that sound. It was the wind from an arrow piercing the air. It punctured Tic-Tac's back. Tic-Tac fell to the floor. A girl screamed at the far end of the jungle. Abe knew that cry better than he knew the rush of the arrow, the pitiful yell that gurgled out from the heart and almost strangled him once, when he had found Elise on the floor drained of life. No one but Sarah could have made that cry.

Abe turned to Kelsey. "Did you make that?" he whispered. No nod, no sign, no response was answer enough. She signaled the arrow. They couldn't turn back now.

IMMINENT LOSS

JAMES

ARAH'S SCREAM RANG HARSHER AND TRUER THAN ANY sound James had heard in a long time—since he recalled his friend's scream for a similar reason, when he and Abe could still call each other friends, but that had changed long ago in a place where time was nothing more than a difference between light and dark. Seasons didn't matter, weeks and months and years didn't matter. What mattered changed with the day, between when the light first shined and the night started to spread. Sometimes happiness came, but now it seemed to only come with a price.

Tic-Tac lay in the shadow, his face pressed into

the snow with a shattered sound of another good one gone young. James tried to hold Sarah back but the scream held everyone in place, unsure or unaware or just plain amazed at the raw sound of someone breaking. She broke through James's arms and ran for the limp back of Tic-Tac where the stiff arrow in his body stood out more than his frame in the snow. Charlotte held on tight to Autry and told her everything would be okay. Autry wiped her eyes and said she was tired. James wanted so much to go back to the days some time ago when Max and Danny pissed on the snow and made snow cones, gave one to Nan and one to Ash and told them they had found lemon-flavored syrup in the stash from the ship. That night Ash and Nan repaid Danny and Max by throwing a bucket full of fresh asparagus piss on the heating vents, making that pungent scent steam through their room while Danny and Max ran out screaming and stinking of sharpness that stuck to their skin for days. James laughed in the way that hurt his stomach so much he thought he would cramp up and throw up.

Sarah hovered over Tic-Tac, Charlotte stood over Autry, and Abe stood silent in the distance as the torches on the horizon faded away. A howl went through the air closer than what James had heard in a long time. In succession, one, then two, then four, then more, it was a storm that swirled around them all. Running away from the faded lights came the calls and the blast of dogs, down from their perches or their caves, wherever their den was, and onto the impromptu battlefield the jungle had become. The frozen silence turned to terror as both parties realized no one was safe because dogs didn't discriminate on whom they attacked.

The large pack broke through the trees and the disembodied howls turned into sharp teeth and foaming mouths. Abe's armament was ready, turning their spears and arrows on the feral group. The outliers weren't prepared for the burst of rabid packs—not Abe's, not the dogs'.

"We have to find some way to stick together," Charlotte said.

"We have to find a way out of here," James said.

"Can you get Sarah?"

She continued to hover over Tic-Tac in the wake of charging dogs. She gripped the tall stick that protruded from Tic-Tac, rocking and pulling the arrow from his limp body. James ran to her as the outliers tried to run away, herded now by Charlotte who kept hold of Autry's hand.

"We need to go," James said.

"Not without him," Sarah said. The arrow was out, stuck between her fists. She refused to let go; she held onto something that might bring her closer to Tic-Tac in his final moments, James thought.

"I'm not dead yet," Tic-Tac said in a gentle yell.

"Holy shit, dude," James said. "Dogs!"

"Help me up," Tic-Tac said.

The tumult started fast and noisy with the dogs busting through the tree line that once stood like a wall, guarding the outliers and pushing them through one way or another. None of the settlement ran. Some kids yelled, filled with the thrashing rush of adrenaline that made the heart almost burst with excitement, James remembered. But he didn't want to be anywhere near the fight, whether with dogs or with the settlement. Teagan ran toward Tic-Tac wielding a knife.

"Where's Autry!" he screamed. "You took my sister!"

"I was trying to keep her safe!" Tic-Tac said.

James tripped Teagan and his knife fell out of his hands. James smothered Teagan to the ground and said, "She's safe. She's with Charlotte." Teagan squirmed but James didn't release him. "She's over there." James pointed and they saw Autry running away from the fray.

"Go with her," Tic-Tac said.

"Don't forget your knife," James said. He stood and helped Teagan up. Teagan picked up his knife and ran to Autry, disappearing behind the trees. James and Sarah helped Tic-Tac and made their stretch away from the dogs. Behind them came a snarl. James told Sarah to continue on, wrapping Tic-Tac's arms around her shoulders.

"What about you?" Tic-Tac asked. James didn't answer. He turned around and saw the sharp teeth and falling drool from the rabid dog, gray and powdery white. Behind it he watched the swarm of the pack take down one person after another; the pack was its strength, able to encircle one or two people and attack their prey hard. Some settlers speared some dogs, the sharp yelps of the animals cracking through the battle roars. The dog in front of James smelled like decay; it had probably eaten in the last few days and the meat rotted in its teeth. James made himself as big as possible, with his hands in the air. The dog growled his putrid growl; blood drenched its open mouth. James alternated between clapping his hands and stepping backwards, barking at the dog as the dog leaked rancid drool on the snow. The dog stepped toward James. James stepped toward the dog with his hands in the air. The dog stepped back. They danced back and forth to show dominance. James couldn't see behind him. He needed to keep his eyes on the dog. He didn't know if he would step on a branch and fall to the ground. He didn't know if the outliers had escaped or not. He could barely see the battle fought in front of him where bodies of dogs and kids fell on and over one another in drifting rivers of blood. Instead he found the harsh reality that anyone on the ground, dog or person, was dead.

The dog barked. James stepped forward and yelled. The dog yelped and dropped. An arrow struck through its ribs and James watched the animal die in a wisp of pain that stung James because he didn't want the animal to die. But at the last second of the dog's life James knew that it had come to one or the other, him or the dog. Abe stood in the chaos with a lifted bow, empty of arrows, aimed in James's direction. His gloves were off and a single black-tipped finger stood out against the bow's pale wood.

Abe's skin was pale, his finger moldy, decrepit, about to turn; *just like the rest of him.*

Was that arrow meant for the dog or James? The flames in Abe's eyes were unmistakable, almost lighting up the entire jungle in the darkness of the now-gone torches. He didn't wait to find out and never wanted to know. He turned and ran along the path that Charlotte had taken, hoping he wouldn't be followed by either pack he left behind.

COMING HOME

JAMES

JAMES FOUND THE OUTLIERS IN AN UNGUARDED CAVE THAT carved into the foothills of the volcano, somehow hidden from them all before. There was a small yip and yelp in the depths that echoed along the walls.

"We're not alone!" Phil yelled. He took out his bow and arrow and aimed it into the cave's depths. A small pack of pups littered the cave. More outliers recoiled. "Let's just finish this." The pups barked and growled at Phil. They jumped forward and back.

"Stop," Charlotte said. Her voice was tame and tired. She pushed Phil's bow down. "They're puppies." Charlotte stepped closer to the dogs and brought Autry with her, taking small, calculated steps toward the pups. Charlotte got to her knees, took off her gloves, and put out her hand. The earlier growls subsided. Two of the pups nuzzled against her fingers and licked her palm, taking the moisture and the salt from her skin. The rest of the pups followed with excited barks, climbing over one another in the cavern. Six in the litter greeted the rest of the outliers. Phil replaced the bow and arrow. He even smiled at the pups.

Tic-Tac sat against the wall. "I'll be fine," he told Sarah who stood over him like a guardian, a desperate mother, a hurt lover, someone who just wanted to make sure he would do as he said and be okay.

"I guess this is home," James said. "At least for now."

"It doesn't look so bad," Charlotte said. The pups continued to run around the outliers, excited for the attention. Charlotte took Franklin out of the bag and placed him near the wall.

"Nice hands," James said. "Couldn't have been easy holding onto him."

"You always hold on to the things you care about," she said.

"That a fact?"

They looked around the cave and found their world—their family—exploring the depths of the earthen walls. The air was warmer than it had been in the ship. Every voice resounded a bit against the ceiling, but they could be happy here, James thought, for now. The pups yipped. More and more outliers settled in, finding comfort on the floor. Autry had already fallen asleep with a gray pup nestled into her crossed arms.